QUARANTINE

As Experienced Through the eyes of an Octogenarian

John K. Spitzberg

QUARANTINE
AS EXPERIENCED THROUGH THE EYES OF AN OCTOGENARIAN

iUniverse books may be ordered through booksellers or by contacting:

iUniverse
1663 Liberty Drive
Bloomington, IN 47403
www.iuniverse.com
844-349-9409

ISBN: 978-1-6632-3038-6 (sc)
ISBN: 978-1-6632-3039-3 (e)

Library of Congress Control Number: 2021921039

Print information available on the last page.

iUniverse rev. date: 12/30/2021

Contents

Foreword

This is a book primarily written for elders who are closing in on living a century. All others read at your own risk.

It is a story about an octogenarian who finds himself locked up in a small hotel room in the middle of London by the government of Great Britain in quarantine for twelve days due to Covid-19. I do not suggest that younger, fitter, and more active people are excluded from reading this story, but the material will best be understood and appreciated by those who are in their 70's, 80's and perhaps 90's. I do not want youngsters to gag, become bored and wish that they had heeded this warning. However, anyone with parents, grandparents or even a great grandparent will hopefully find this book worthy of their time, at least to get a glimpse of what is in their future and what their elderly loved ones might be experiencing.

Quarantine was never meant to be on David's itinerary, but neither was Covid-19 meant to become this century's worse medical nightmare (so far). A famous Buddhist monk from England but residing in Udon Thani, Thailand in discussing the horrendous Tsunami in the South Indian Ocean on December 26, 2004, said something to the effect that "Shit happens. Now get on with life." He didn't use this gauche language, but the point was made clearly. His words spoken in English made a profound impression on me and helped to calm the anxiety of so many of us who went to Thailand to be of help after a quarter of a million souls were lost. The pandemic has killed and maimed millions and in India shows no indication of halting horrible ravishes yet. Each day bodies pile up for burial and line the streets and roadways in many towns and villages. India has surpassed the United States in deaths per day. Welcome to the world's largest democracies. I live in Alaska. Not only are we the largest state, have the highest mountain in North America, but now have the most cases of Covid per capita in the U.S.A.

Unlike someone trying to blame the Chinese or Evangelicals attempting to relate the Covid Virus to the Book of Revelations and end of days in the Christian bible or even economist, David Malthus explaining population control by war, disease, or starvation as a means of thinning out the population, as in fact it has, it does little good to dwell on why, but to accept the carnage and get on with life. In no way does it mean that saving as many lives as possible is not called for and that science, vaccinations, and testing are to be abandoned or made fun of, but together with following health and science guidelines, this too will pass or it will destroy the planet like climate change.

It is with this in mind that I decided to share the experiences of an octogenarian, David Green. He wants to combat cabin fever by getting away from his little house in Alaska. When he gets to London, he is quarantined in a hotel room in the Kings Cross area of Euston Road for thirteen days. Talk about cabin fever.

I think there is truth that behind all non-fiction there is imagination, and the converse is also true. In all fiction there is truth lingering somewhere in the background. It seems many people spend a lifetime looking for truth, an elusive pursuit. Your life, your experiences will be helpful in determining what is true and what is not. Additionally, I hope you subscribe to the cliché, "I may not agree with what you say, but I'll die defending your right to say it." Lots of what is in this book is up for disagreement, debate, and personal interpretation.

David Green was introduced to the reading community in two books, the first being Doing it the Hard Way and its sequel Kelly House.

He is a figment of my old brain with lapses, forgetfulness, and warped sense of humor. But David is real in some ways also. He is a composite of many elders, mostly men but some of the fairer sex as well.

To me, he represents so many aspects of growing old, so many, many moments of lucidity followed by brain warp and insane forgetfulness, such as forgetting his grandchild's name, where he is, when he is to meet someone, who he is supposed to join for what meal and how to get from point A to B as examples. For instance, name recognition, chronological mistakes, thinking processes, all lead to swaths of fallacy and even blatant lies, misrepresentations, and embarrassing realities. Indeed, there are the physical propensities for falling, becoming light- headed, disorientation, and sensing an upheaval in the upper and lower areas of the stomach which can be very embarrassing especially when in fact the community is experiencing mild earthquakes. David has often heard rumblings which he attributes to something he ate or devoured too quickly only to read something on Facebook from someone in the community asking about the shaking of her home.

David's self- assessment of his physical, psychological, and social acceptance of his lot in life may throw the reader into a dither, but no less than it does him. He lives it day in and day out and he has just experienced another twirl of the big wheel of life. Furthermore, David is addicted to the Gestalt Prayer by famed Gestalt therapist Fritz Perls who died many years ago. It goes:

> *I do my thing and you do your thing. I am not in this world to live up to your expectations, and you are not in this world to live up to mine. You are you, and I am I, and if by chance we find each other, it is beautiful and if not, it cannot be helped.*

Younger readers may be in shock at the words David utters about issues like bathroom habits, fleeting memories of sexual pleasures long ago, perhaps not talked about in polite company but shared openly in Quarantine. Yes, the stream of consciousness is played with frequently, joyously and in some passages with glee, excitement, and passion but also with abject sadness and despondency, and in some cases concurrently or sequentially. And is this not what life is all about? You be the judge.

And why not? This is a book by elders for and about getting old, getting through the 70's, 80's, and if meant to be, the 90's. The book does not venture into those rare beings who live a century or more. The author has seen pictures of celebrating birthday parties for centurions, but it seems the only ones who know what is going on are those throwing the party, not those for whom the party is thrown. Of course, there are exceptions to every rule. I would not want my dear friends who are in their 90's to become insulted over a slight not meant. Nor do I wish to be excluded from their party. I love to sing Happy Birthday to loved ones and acquaintances alike. Additionally, I may reach the century mark and I want my cake and ice cream too!

Gerontologists, those who study us may find some nuggets of information here of use in their work, but I doubt it. This is fiction, after all. Younger readers may use the book as a reference on how to deal with dear old Gramps or the equivalent for the female version of "Gramps"? Some may become ill at the suggestion that 80-year-olds could have moments of sexual fantasy or must mop up after themselves when they have an "accident", like a puppy or incontinence like their best four-legged friend who has given them years of joy, unconditional love and, placed them on a pedestal that no human belongs upon. Or young people may vehemently denounce the book as having no relevance to anything they will ever have to experience...Afterall, youth shouldn't have to concern themselves with what their twilight years will bring them, at least not for fifty or sixty years. So they can say, "It will never happen to me."

I have tried to share as much reality about Covid-19 as possible, not falsehoods, or insane ideas about drinking Clorox, or some other potion to kill the germs in one's body. What a political mess we have experienced over this pandemic, and it is still alive and well. I freely admit that I cannot keep up with the changes, testing requirements, and or vaccination themes. I am no Dr. Anthony Fauci or any of his cohorts.

I am not Dr. Sanjay Gupta on CNN with his deep concern, grave facial expressions, and breaks for commercial advertisements just before he announces an earth-shattering new statistic, breakthrough, or some other dire happening. It leaves me furious that Capitalism rears its ugly head even in this pandemic. To be sure, people have found ways to capitalize on the Virus, to make money, but many more have lost their livelihood, their homes, possessions, and self-respect as well. "Isms" should play no role in this horror. Stop reading for a moment and think about this.

Falling into the Quarantine trap in London and having to endure invasive tests to find the slimy virus hiding in the mucus folds of one's pharynx or the cavities of the nostrils below the base of the skull apply to young and old alike, but knowing that death among elderly, often lonely nursing home residents outweighs the demise of youth by some gigantic statistical percentage is heart breaking for so many family members who never get to say goodbye or kiss Nanna or Popa for the last time. It brings tears to my eyes just writing this.

Do not assume that I am a Socialist, Communist, Feudalist, Mercantilist, or any other economic variation of the above groups. I am not saying that TV is all hype to sell products. I am also not saying that the anchors on all the channels be they left, right or center bow to their sponsors and the hell with the news for getting in the way although some do. Sometimes it is infuriating. The anchors and newsmen and women have families, loved ones, and some have been bitten by Covid-19 themselves and have been extremely sick as a result of it. I can just hear some younger person saying, "Don't mind him. He's just losing it and ranting." Maybe yes, maybe not and if so, it can't be helped.

However, this book has links to another theme and one that Henry Miller, the man who wrote Tropic of Capricorn and other Avant Guard novels years ago may well have appreciated. It makes an attempt to share elements of elder sexuality that may seem gross to young people, make middle-age people blush just thinking about their parents in bed together and bring tears of loneliness and other emotional states to octogenarians.

David comes face to face with his brain's shutdown of anything remotely connected to sexuality. I remember that my dad told me that when he stopped having sex with his lady friends after the death of my mom, he stopped wanting to date, socialize with widows and other elderly women. This extended to not trying to dress up, make efforts to smell fresh or any other desires related to dating and sharing a bed.

For him, it was all about the ability to "perform". I think he was about 85, maybe 86 when he entered this new phase of life or chapter, which lasted until he died at the age of 97. For 12 more years, he progressed from independent to assisted living and finally total dependency with a young Haitian woman attending to all his needs. Well, not all, but somehow, he began to think of her as a wife and spoke of her and to her with endearing words. She took everything he said with an understanding smile and realized that Dad's brain was losing its ability to decipher truth from fiction, love object from professional concern. She was so good to him and took care of his bodily needs until the end.

I was not living in Florida those final years and my son, Jerry had to call me in Missoula, Montana one evening crying that grandpa died in his sleep at the nursing home. When Natasha came to work, she found him or maybe someone performing a security check did. As I write this my heart is heavy with sorrow. A tinge of guilt still haunts me. I spent so little time with Dad as he prepared to leave this world for another which he believed in as a Reform Jew. I, on the other hand, believe that we live on in the living, the good, the bad and the ugly. Upon death, we simply cease to exist… I can live with this belief system as long as I exist; I will not worry about it after I no longer am. Heaven and hell are figments of the imagination, and religious zealots use them to control people. I think people don't need to be threatened or bribed to be good and worthwhile human beings. I am a Humanist, Ethical Culturists, and a citizen of the world. It is enough for me.

So Quarantine is written in the here and now, but my father's life, especially his social life after Mom's death wends its way in a collage of so many lives particularly David's into the fabric of the tale. Dad never had to live through or die due to Covid-19. He never became a statistic. He died years before the first hint of the monster in our midst.

That part of the saga is David's alone. Unlike my father, David would not live a sedentary life. Reading a newspaper from front to back would never interest David. Nor having the television blaring hour upon hour through long naps. Visits from Jerry and the grandchildren, plus occasional visits from the house physician, cardiologist who checked his pacemaker, social worker, and maintenance men who checked all the appliances, security gismos and whatever needed fixing would not be on David's agenda. Eating in a quasi-elegant dining room day in and day out long after he no longer tasted the food because he paid for it as part of the room and board given by the elderly care home was not for David.

Was it because I was adopted and did not share Dad's hereditary traits, characteristics, intelligence, and DNA? Was nature stronger than nurture? Actually, I am nothing like my biological father was either.

Lastly, this forward is being written or scribbled on a bus as the coach responds to every pothole, sudden deceleration by the driver and crying of a baby or two sitting to my rear. After quarantine, David decided to see two places in England he never saw when he first came to London back in the last century. This part of the saga belongs to me as well as David. For the line between David and this author blurs and sharpens from time to time. We are both octogenarians. What do you expect? Life happens. Now get on with it!

Acknowledgement

I wish to thank the following people for having read or listened to pages and/or chapters of this account. All of them were younger than I, and they read and listened at their own risk. I appreciate their literary criticism, frank evaluation, and willingness to give of their time and advice. I am older than all of them and have learned from each one something about writing, myself and life in general.

Billy Bartee

Brett Benson

Dave Smith

Dede Donavan

Diane Langeler

Dwayne Beals

Francis Hunter

George McCann

Janice Smith

Jean Grenning

Jeff Spitzberg

Jerry Spitzberg

Judy Moss

Julie Benson

Miriam Osredkar

Noah Bettineski

Roy Hunter

Selma LaBrecquet Hawk

Steve Renke

Sue Stollen

Wayne Hawk

CHAPTER 1

No Place to Go, just a Mirror for Company.

David Green didn't like what he saw in the mirror. He felt his left forearm, then his right, saw the folds, sagging, irregular, blotched spots on his arms, and then vainly felt his pecks and frowned. Where was the muscle that was supposed to be there and used to be? His left arm was stronger than the right. Or was that his imagination? Closing both hands, stiff, pain in the joints, unable to form a fist due to frost bite, arthritis, tissue build up in the forefinger on his left hand from sticking his hand into Chucky's mouth in a dog fight to the finish. A trigger finger on his left hand seemed to have a life of its own. Painful yes, but a gentle thump of his palm just below the finger and the finger righted itself in a snap to attention. All this and only 83 years young. David smiled. It could be worse- right? "I could be an invalid in a wheelchair."

He dared not look down at his manhood which was barely visible in the mirror. He couldn't count the number of times he cursed it as though it had a mind of its own. In a fit of anger, he threatened to turn it in for a new one. He thought about a website for old men with lost manhood. Again the fear that he was the only one affected crossed his mind and he laughed. It wasn't a common point of discussion and he doubted that many old men stood around lamenting their losses, especially not this one.

David suddenly remembered his favorite movie, Moon Struck with Cher and Nicholas Cage so many years ago. The grandfather with his five dogs who lived in the old two-story huge mansion with his son, daughter-in-law, and granddaughter, (Cher) would take his dogs for walks. He met with other Italian elderly men in a cemetery where the dogs urinated on the graves of others who were not so lucky to be able to talk to their friends, at least not in this world. David doubted that the topic they reminisced about in Italian, of course, was lost manhood.

Why not? It preoccupied him. Why not them? Unless, unless they hadn't lost their desires, their fantasies or ability to make their wives, if alive, tingle inside if not more. In comedy Moon Struck touched on elder sexuality and desire. The scenes between Loretta (Cher) and her father are precious. The movie is worth seeing for this topic if nothing else.

When David was in a hurry, the pool of urine on the floor and the smell of it on his outer garment infuriated him and he swore at his penis with a vengeance and the same question flooded his brain, "Is that all there is?" He ignored the words of his urologist that all he needed to do was lose some weight and miraculously he would be the man he once was… Fat chance! Then he laughed again at his use of the word "fat".

Now he could really give some time to figuring out how to protect himself from needing a diaper. Glancing out the window of his imprisonment the Brits called Quarantine, David gazed upon the droplets of freezing rain splashing on the garden roof, which was never used, at least as long as he had been in the room. His view included King Cross Street Underground Station and the old castle of red/orange brick to its left, sea gulls flapping their wings with vengeance as they fought the winds and floated by his window, and people scurrying hither and yonder to avoid the raindrops falling almost laterally upon their heads was all he saw and nothing else.

He could see heads of children spin when a nasty gust of wind slapped them. Most clutched to their moms and dads, but a few ran ahead as if to say "I'm all grown up now. I don't need you to hold my hand." Parents ran to protect their offspring anyway. The sight was beautiful, and he felt a lump in his throat. He saw young girls and boys hugging, their clothes blowing in the winds and dresses rising above the girl's knees sometimes exposing panties. He sighed.

David looked to see if anyone was playing chess across the street at the Underground station under the eaves but saw no one doing so. He might have broken his quarantine and snuck over to challenge a Brit to a game. One day he took a solidary walk past a park and a bunch of Black, white bearded men were sitting on the lawn or lazing on the benches sipping from bags. He doubted they were drinking tea. There, too, had they been slouched over a chess board he would have broken his vows of isolation to offer a challenge. He, of course, would be masked, incognito as the best mediocre pawn pusher on the Continent. Wait, wait, David wasn't on the Continent. He was in England separated by the channel.

But no vows were broken that day and no challenge to his mediocrity would ensue. No, he would be mostly confined to his postage stamp room, his mirror which hid nothing, and sporadic ventures from it while he obeyed the rules of quarantine set by Boris' medical experts.

A few years ago David had lots of friends, non-better than those in Asheville, North Carolina at Kelly House, a commune for seniors who loved to create prose, art, poetry, and all imaginations of the heart. From time to time, he dreamt of the Appalachians and their soft, well rounded peaks weathered by centuries of rain, snow, sun and wearing down. Some mavens said these were the oldest mountains in the world. All David could think of was the beautiful, rounded breasts of women he had bedded in his life. As he aged, he thought more about the majesty of the rolling hills, not the women he had sex with. Another reminder of getting old and a tinge of sadness. He often wondered about monogamous men and women who slept with only one person. He both admired them and thought about how much they missed.

Twenty-five years ago more or less the old man lived in Pompano Beach, Florida and could see a light house, bright lights welcoming the yachts of the rich into safe moorings in the harbor on the Intercostal. He sighed just thinking about it while looking out his Tower of London like window. Joy, sadness brought on by memories, oh so long ago, and suddenly a new memory interrupted his past and he thought of a woman he'd just met three days before who said he looked a bit like Ernest Hemingway. David thought about Hemingway and a fleeting thought of Ernest sticking the barrel under his chin in Idaho and pulling the trigger and he shuddered. Why did people end their own lives? So many veterans, so many years in front of them. Why? Feeling his heart sink into his stomach, the idea was never far removed from his mind when he thought of things he had done to his wives and his leaving his children with his first wife who was dead now from cancer so many years ago.

He looked in the mirror and saw another imperfection. Just below his chin, a pouch like he'd seen in seagulls and pelicans. He flexed his facial muscles ten times hoping to see the pouch disappear, but no, still there. Again he laughed at himself and realized he could swallow live fish and save them in his pouch for dinner later.

His grandma used to say that European women with double chins were opulent, not her words. She had a fifth-grade education and was born in Austria. But David found security in her ample bosom, flabby arms, and unconditional love for him. She'd raised him while his mom worked for the war effort in D.C. at one of the many government offices off Constitution and Independence Avenues.

They'd lived in a tiny apartment in N.W. Washington across the street from an elementary School. Times were tough with the war effort and rationing of food stuffs. David held Grandma's hand while they waited in line for food twice a week. Rain, shine, snow cold or heat, no matter. Bread, butter, meat and on good days vegetables were there for the taking. David was poor but didn't know that he was.

Tears came easy to the old man. As he thought about his youth, suddenly he looked out of his window and shivered. He sighed and remembered the old woman who loved him unconditionally like no one else ever had or ever would. His sadness almost overwhelmed him.

Grandma was dead now, so many years ago. He never really knew his grandfather from Germany. He'd died on December 28, 1938, the same day that his third wife was born. But a mysterious box of letters proved that Julius loved his precious only grandchild. Over the years his mother painted a picture of her father which remained to the present day. Maybe the face in the mirror was his grandfather's.

David thought about the voice of the woman who told him he looked a bit like Hemingway. Her voice was a mixture of English, French and Turkish. She'd been raised in Istanbul, France and traveled widely in her youth. She was immensely proud of her invitation to the Cannes Film Festival to show her art, literary proficiency, and craft.

She'd beem married to a well-known English artist who'd died some years ago. This literary femme was in London to show her late husband's work and sell some at auction. Somehow, she reminded David of homeless elderly women who he'd seen in the alleys behind the apartment when he was a little boy.

They wore black and pillaged through garbage cans and took what they wanted. These women were from the old country and had known hardships. They were products of their past. Even in the New World, old habits were hard to break, and memories only faded, never completely disappeared.

Simone's hair was disheveled, and she wore black pants and a black hoody top. It was the voice though that he could not forget. It was sonorous, yet gravelly in a way which made him think that she might have smoked heavily long ago. She was full of herself, her contribution to the arts presently and as a young woman. David gave her his card and she did the same. Theirs was a short- lived friendship which he suspected would end the moment she returned to her home in another part of the country. He was quite sure she'd throw his card in the rubbish bin when she got home. Perhaps he was projecting his ambivalence.

If she heard anything he said, he doubted it. It was all about her problems, her fear of having been defrauded by a woman who had her late husband's paintings. But she listened intently when David talked about Hemingway, who she swooned over and claimed to have read everything he ever wrote. David told her about the way he'd get people drunk, fighting amongst themselves, and then he'd write his adventurous stories based on their interactions. He loved the movie, Hemingway and Gelhorn about their tempestuous love affair, reporting on the Spanish Revolution and their passion, anger, and her jealousy of his success over her lack of it.

The old man also told her that he'd met one of Ernest Hemingway's friends who'd been an American, Brooklynese, Jewish bullfighter. As an older gentleman he made a small amount of money in Mexico City showing people around, taking them to the fights, and allowing patrons to buy him tequila while he remonstrated about his life with the great literary giant called Papa by his adoring fans. Imagine yourself sitting across the table from the great Sidney Franklin and devouring every word about his life in the ring, as a friend of Hemingway's and Martha Gellhorn in the Spanish Civil War against the Fascistas and with the Wobblies, Lincoln Brigade and Republican Army. Later David did some research on Franklin and found that he'd sympathized with the dictator Franco for some crazy reason and may have been a homosexual in his youth. And once again, David thought of the absurdities of life and the human proclivity for creative lifestyles.

David faced two merciless foes, the new Covid and his old nemesis Type 2 Diabetes. Sugar lows always brought fear to his heart with symptoms and signs getting worse by the minute if he did not eat something with sugar or take some glucose tablets. In paramedic school, they taught that the brain was the only organ of the body that absolutely required sugar or else he would feel feint, clammy, and a fear of impending disorientation. If not treated quickly, he could die.

This day he woke about seven in the morning, opened the curtain to check the weather, gaze upon the entrance to the underground and count the days of his unwanted detainment. He looked in the mirror; Who was that looking back at him?

Monday, day eight and his second Covid-19 home test. If negative, he'd be a free man again- released by the Great Britain Health Service- until the next time. David Green doubted that there would ever be a next time. What was the cliché? Fool me once, on you, fool me twice and we share the idiocy, fool me three times, and I am a damn fool. No pity! Memory loss contributed to the bastardization of the cliché. But the gist was there.

In preparation for the trip across the pond, he went to a barber shop in Boca Raton and had them shear his beard and long straggly hair.

What a difference a haircut made. He looked civilized for the first time in months. Finally, his son and daughter-in-law would approve his appearance. They would not have to make excuses to family and friends for the vagabond who visited. It was all in good humor, or was it, but David doubted that he won any approval for his cave man look. They would not have to explain that their father lived in a rural, isolated, and untamed small town in Alaska with his five mutts from all over the behemoth, Last Frontier. On their last night together, David took the family including his grandson's girlfriend to a fine Indian restaurant, and they could be reassured that their Uppah, a Yupik Eskimo word for grandfather, was not just released from some drunk tank or crevice in a mountain.

David wondered what they thought of him after he cut his hair and beard. On one hand, he craved for their love and respect and on the other hand he cherished his identity as a wannabe Alaskan, and that meant looking anyway he wanted and living off the grid far from the lifestyle of suburbia Rat's Mouth, Florida.

The Spanish translation is Boca Raton. David laughed. His son and daughter-in-law hated it when he referred to their home as one in Rat's Mouth or the mouth of the rat. Spanish is a beautiful language, n'est pas? He mused again at mingling French in his thoughts about Boca Raton.

Meticulously, he took the second test out of the little safe in his room. God willing and the creeks don't rise this would be his last test, but he wasn't going to bet on it. He called 119, the abbreviated phone number on the last page of the test materials.

The Brits were so exacting with instructions for each possible piece of information. Finally, he contacted a living, breathing, voice, this one not from the Scottish Highlands. Thank something or another for small favors. After ten or twenty minutes of going through the same identification he did each time he called, he finally arranged for the young woman to do her magic with the system and sign him up for taking the test.

Everything had to be spelled at least two times using simple words to make sure that every letter was correct. The letter "R" was Romeo, "S" Sierra and "T" Tango. "W" stood for whisky and "X", Xray.

No mistakes, please God (David doubted that any higher power cared whether he and the young telephone worker communicated properly or not.) or everything would have to be started over again. She used technological lingo foreign to the old man and he had to ask her to speak slowly, define some of her words, and treat him like a three-year- old. Words like bar code, abbreviations, he knew not, and specific time frames had to be repeated more than once. And then he was on his own.

First, he cut the swab stick to the exact size so that it would fit into the plastic vial filled three quarters of the way with a murky liquid, and then put the wooden stick into the vial after he swabbed his throat where his tonsils used to be.

The booklet used the term torch and David figured that was the Brits way of saying flashlight. Four swabs on each side of the throat, and oh yes, wash your hands, blow your nose first, and cough into a tissue so excess mucus does not spoil the test. Then stick the cotton ball at the end of the swab up your nose about 2.5cm (1 inch) or until one feels some resistance without perforating your brain stem.

Before starting the self-swab induction, David measured one inch and winced as he had on the first test on the second day of his confinement and momentarily wished that he'd stayed home and taken a couple of days to Seward or Homer in Alaska.

Finally, he stuck the dark yellow mucus covered swab or whatever he gathered in the tube full of the liquid, placed a small absorbent pad in the plastic bag and carefully removed a sealant and closed the bag. He squeezed air out of it first as instructed and went about following the assembly instructions on the return box. The last thing he did was to apply a security seal as directed.

It occurred to him that one false move, one innocent mistake and he could spend the rest of his life in his tiny room in the inn, staring at the mirror, a prisoner in quarantine for life.

Then dressed, ready to transport his test to the laboratory, he left the hotel, but not before searching for the health department undercover cops just itching to fine him for leaving his cell.

Even this endeavor had its problems. On day two of his ordeal, he'd assumed that he should go to the closest post office and mail the parcel to the proper lab. When he made his way in the queue to the postal clerk, he was greeted with a "NO, NO, not here. You must take the test to such and such a street and give it to them".

"Ok, and where is this street and which building do I go to?"

He may have been from India, Pakistan, or New York. Anyway, he took pity on David and scribbled the name of a building on the paper while pointing to the door and telling him to go left out of the post office and look for a big building with a name like Hulu or something of the sort. David found the building about two or three blocks from the post office and found a door with a porter sitting at a desk.

"No, no not here! You must go around the corner and there will be somebody at the door for you." He ushered David out of the building as though the old man had a box of Anthrax or Botulism in his hands. It felt like he should be wearing a HASMAT suit and that he had violated some British law by walking into the building in just a jacket and hoody with a mask, of course. In the past anyone with a mask was considered a criminal or bank robber. Now if you entered a bank without a mask, they called the police. Whole new meaning to masked bank robbery.

He turned the corner and found the end of the edifice and turned right. To his right was a small door and a man sitting on a chair beyond a glass enclosed window with a small opening just big enough for the Covid-19 test. He motioned to put the test in the slot and drop it into a box. David had an image of the liquid falling out of the vial as he dropped the box in, even though he made sure that it was tight and fully insulated by the plastic bag with the absorbent pad. The diminutive man made no move to touch it, to check to see if all rules and instructions were followed. Then he bade a sorrowful "Goodbye." And that was it.

The Alaskan swore to himself that he seen a movie like this and pictured a clandestine drop of some sort of a Double 007 caper.

Anticlimactical, but with David's imagination he ran with it. Truly he believed that this entire process was a scam. He pictured the government and Boris Johnson himself having gone to great lengths to isolate foreigners, even those who had not broken away from the empire some three hundred years before. "This will teach those insolent colonists!"

A ton of questions entered his brain, but the fellow behind the screen showed no interest in being of help. David was summarily dismissed without another word.

Almost trotting back to his room, he called 119 again, went through the same identification process with another young lady who exuded an anxiousness to be helpful. David recounted his experiences leaving out the invasion of his larynx and base of his brain. His relief was palpable when she told him that what he experienced was indeed proper and she offered to document that he had done his first test and that in about three days he would know the results of the test and be ever that closer to the end of his sentence. She meant his quarantine. "Three days, my god, I could be dead from Covid by then."

The next morning, or to be exact Day 3 of his State enforced incarceration David had a knock on his door. Standing before him was a young, strapping Black man who'd been sent to make sure that there had been no escape, no untoward action on David's part, and no attempt to swim the English Channel to escape his imprisonment.

Groggily, David answered questions which he didn't entirely understand, but the gist of them was along concern for David's well - being, experiences from the day before, and generally meant to help the old guy negotiate any hurdles, pitfalls, or problems that the young man could be helpful with. He assured David that if he couldn't help or answer his questions, he would speak with his supervisor and that maybe another person might be sent.

To David, it only meant that he'd better not leave the premises for longer than an hour at a time or he might be heavily fined for breaking quarantine and perhaps even arrested, tried, and sentenced to prison for what- David was not sure. But he was traumatized enough to remain locked in his room with only the mirror to talk to, to commiserate with and share sad looks. He laughed, "Mirror, mirror on the wall."

There was a TV in the room, but he was determined not to turn it on. TV, in his opinion, was an opiate of the people perhaps as Marx had meant it. He wasn't sure, but one thing was certain. He watched too much CNN, MSNBC and his beloved Special Victims Unit, NYPD programming. He'd come to love the characters on the cop shows and yet saw the brutality which the police used at times even in made for TV scripts.

Didn't they realize that was proof pudding that some, not all, not most, but some cops thought they were above the law and human rights of all human beings? At least SVU addressed the abuse, but the stories about police work in Chicago did not even attempt to address police brutality, at least not on the shows David watched.

He thought it odd that producers, directors, and those who paid big bucks for advertising allowed this police abuse on the shows. In light of the killing of George Floyd and so many other Black and Brown people who were treated very differently than Caucasian citizens were, why were they not more sensitive?

So far, he'd stuck by his rule not to watch any television during this period of detainment. He read a lot and even managed to finish an excellent book about the Nationalizing of the Christian Right in America.

The author called it Christian Nationalism. David would find a way to write about the book, its hypothesis and what the author saw as the future of the country. Of course, Trump was out; Biden was in and for this David gave conditional thanks. Biden was too tied to business as usual for the quarantined old man.

But somewhere he'd read that that Democrats were so involved in political and human correctness that they talked a lot but accomplished little. Biden was a good man; Trump was a vile and obnoxious horror show. David questioned whether Biden's commitment to doing good would suffice to keep America from heading toward a second civil war.

Day 8, of his ordeal and repeating the Covid-19 test one last time, fingers crossed. He showered, thinking that the best part of his accommodations was the shower. Hot water, plenty of it and warmth from the electrical heating system in each room was a novelty which, in his house, in Alaska was not fully functional. There a shower was always followed by goose bumps, cold and a rush to towel off and jump into bed with the covers over his head. This, true even in the summer.

The old man even bought some Gillette blades and shaved. He hadn't shaven in eight or nine months. But the more he gazed at himself in the mirror, the more he liked his face, the other parts of his body not so much.

CHAPTER 2

Negative, Vaccinated and Good to Go

The hard part of this ordeal began yesterday. Waiting for the results of the second test was a nail biter. What if it's positive? What then? Already the Veterans Administration had stuck two shots of vaccine in his arm. They used Moderna.

Didn't seem to matter to the Brits. Test, test and more testing were their concern, not the fact that he was already vaccinated. It seemed like a new industry had been invented and beware the poor tourist.

Shrugging, he went on writing and every now and then peering out of his window which wouldn't open. He realized that the roof of the exchange was what he thought was a roof garden. In his time in quarantine, the pound went down from 68 to 67 to the dollar. Britain had returned to the pound and left the European Union's currency behind.

This ordeal really began in Florida when he visited his family. American Airlines demanded a negative Covid test within 48 hours of travel just to get on the plane. Finding a test site wasn't all that difficult and a friend of his son's took him over to the urgent care facility about a mile from their home. Some nice young girl did the vitals, pronounced David alive and within normal limits for his age bracket.

Then a stern, masked, and gowned woman arrived with a swab, vial, and attacked his nostrils with a passion. She, too, seemed to be aiming for his brain stem, but stopped before any blood came spewing out of his nose and throat.

Within a half hour he was given a negative rapid test result and it was signed by a physician, perhaps the director of the urgent care clinic. With paper in hand, he was ready to go to England and then anticipated leaving immediately for North Africa and Humphrey Bogart's Casablanca. Little did he know that he would be jailed in London, and it would be called quarantine...

The first test on his second day of quarantine took three days to come back negative and what a relief that was. David called 119 again and made sure that the woman or was it a man recorded the results, and that David was still on track to complete his sentence.

There was so much ambivalence connected with this quarantine business. Although he joked about it in his head, he knew that all countries were affected and each strove to stop the virus at all costs. Too many deaths and now India had regained the lead in morbidity. Lack of oxygen, beds, ventilators and so on, the very same problems which Governor Cuomo pontificated about for days on end on CNN and

MSNBC with lapses for commercials for things like buying new windows, bed sheets, or taking a vacation on a cruise ship.

For a while Cuomo was being discussed as a potential presidential contender until women began to speak out about sexual harassment and his insistence that they sleep with him. No big deal in many parts of the world, but the ME, TOO movement ignited and pity the poor old goat who got caught trying to entice females into uncomfortable positions, literally and figuratively particularly when the old guys had authority over them such as in a work situation or as an elected official.

David realized that he felt some modicum of compassion for Cuomo's plight, an aging, divorced male who was lonely at the top and wanted to revive his sexual life. Mistake number one- "Don't shit under your own flagpole" NEVER!!

But once, just once to his regret, David had done just that in a manner of speaking. After a divorce, he ran into a young woman who'd been a student of his in his night class and feeling lonely, isolated, and craving affection had asked the youth, albeit she was over 19 but he was in his forties, an old man in her eyes to spend time with him.

In no way was she the least bit interested and almost had a meltdown right in front of him. They parted on uncomfortable terms and David swore then and there never to do anything like it again. And he never did, but he had many, many days and nights of loneliness and remorse for years. He wasn't even asking for a sexual liaison, just company. Even this could and would be misconstrued. He vowed never to go out with any woman unless she was withing three years of his age.

This would mean 80-86 years of age presently. Pity the poor 79-year- old. She would be just too young.

He gazed out his window, somber sense of having violated the ME TOO movement which would not become a feminist concept for years to come in the twenty-first century. What the hell was her name? Proof that he didn't at least acknowledge her personhood. What a foul scoundrel he was. Quarantine was not good enough; Hell he deserved the guillotine.

In all fairness how could he complain about his confinement? What was 10, 11 or even more days in the bigger scheme of things? He thought of his elder son, Ari, the Hebrew name for Lion suffering from the effects of the horrid disease. Talking to him on the phone and hearing the terrible hacking cough, the gurgles of mucus forming in his throat and the difficulty at getting each sentence out of his mouth. Already today information on the computer indicated 157,049,132 Cases and 3,274,681 Deaths .... and rising. And he couldn't even be with his son to console and care for him, even if he were in the country.

Maybe Malthus was right and Covid was simply a means generated to control population growth. Thomas Robert Malthus was a famous 18th-century British economist known for the population growth philosophies outlined in his 1798 book "An Essay on the Principle of Population." In it, Malthus theorized that populations would continue expanding until growth is stopped or reversed by disease, famine, war, or calamity. David was fond of going to everyone's common encyclopedia Wikipedia for information he needed. He knew that scholars frowned upon the use of Wikipedia. But then Green was no scholar, just another old man on the street living his life as best he could.

For years David had made no pretense. He was no intellectual, no wise man either in the biblical nor generic sense. Did he yearn to be such? Perhaps, but after all these years, he doubted it would ever come to be. The transliteration for wise men in Hebrew was "Chakkim" and from the time of the writing of the Old Testament, kings called upon the wise for advice, counsel, and clear headedness. This senior citizen always cautioned anyone who asked his opinion to take what he said with caution and concern for accuracy. It could have simply been a means to protect himself from foolish and/or half- baked theory.

Could Covid-19, the 19 simply being the year that the first outbreak was recorded according to every man's bible of knowledge be what Malthus talked about? David read that "on December 31, 2019, the World Health Organization (WHO) was informed of a cluster of cases of pneumonia of unknown cause detected in Wuhan City, Hubei Province, China." Thus, the United States became embroiled in the horrors of a world-wide pandemic, pan meaning all over the globe. People from six of the seven continents and probably all countries in those six land masses became ill, recovered, or died. And some who recovered still have side effects and may for the rest of their lives.

The old guy wondered whether Covid had made its journey to Antarctica. Few tourists ventured there and those who made their life's work as scientists were pretty darn careful in general. Getting sick on Base Camp was no picnic. They'd have to be flown out.

So, he began to think of the last three or four days again. Maybe it was like being paroled and awaiting the day that a suit of clothes, a little money and a bus ticket was given an inmate and then he'd walk out a free (what did that mean?) man.

The wait for the results of the second test came on Wednesday. Yes, yes- Negative Mr. Green. No more worrying that every sniffle, every scratchy throat, and every stomachache meant that he had the Virus.

So he called the hot line, the notorious 119 and went through the tedium of giving his name, birthday, home address, etc., punched the correct dial to be placed on the queue to speak with a live, breathing, thinking human being. Each one of the people he spoke with over the duration of quarantine was friendly, some more informative than others and sympathetic when David told them he didn't know anything about cell phones, advanced jargon like bar code and specialty this's and that's.

Only once did David feel aggravated when the first voice tried to hook him up with another worker and the line went dead. Other worries such as hoping for a Canadian, easily understood Englander or maybe even a South African from the Cape or Pretoria, not usually experienced when speaking to an American over the line were always possible. David gasped when sure enough one of the helpful youthful voices was clearly from the highlands of Scotland. He barely made out his own name and pleaded with him or her to slow down.

This time he was assured that he had completed his quarantine and that he was free to leave the solitary confinement and seek other oldsters to kibbitz with. These were his words, not theirs and in fact he had already spoken to the old gal whose husband left her a house and thousands of pounds worth of artwork.

Over the ten or eleven days he'd gotten to know the hotel employees too. Two or three were from Egypt, two or three from Romania, one from Brazil and another from the Dominican Republic. All stayed securely behind the glass shield constructed to maintain safety away from the guests who like D.G. might be carrying the dreaded death. None of the maître-D's seemed particularly worried and did not badger the guests to wear masks.

He didn't spend excessive amounts of time with them for obvious reasons, but occasionally he'd have long conversations about their countries, how they came to be in England, their families, and what they thought of Trump. The Dominican was a young beautiful black girl who worked as a cleaning woman. David didn't want her to come into his room for lots of reasons, so she left him towels, took out the trash and he did the rest. In her absence, middle-aged Romanian women filled in and did the same for David. Their accents were gruff and their humor almost non- existent. But the comely Dominican smiled, chatted and told David a good deal about herself and her country. It seemed to David that her accent was sort of like a Jamaican/s, lilting, uplifting and melodious. "You are like me gramps, so sweet and how do you say it, charming, yes that's it."

"Well thank you my dear. Perhaps it is because you are so sweet and caring as well." She winked and went off to clean another room. David was cheered by her friendship.

A few nights, a young Iraqi woman about the age of his oldest grandchild sat six to twelve feet from David and spoke to an Egyptian. They spoke Arabic to each other and English to him.

She seemed very bright and yet damaged in some way that David couldn't put his finger on. Perhaps life had already taken a toll on her young life. But, years of working with damaged youth and adults made his ears twitch, thankfully not one of the signs or symptoms of Covid and he spoke to her guardedly and with caution. David did not want a situation of any sort to keep him in confinement one more second than necessary.

He felt that under a veneer of propriety lay an incredibly angry and guarded child. He did not want any untoward incident to happen and especially one where an ambulance or even the police might have to be called.

The first day of freedom and David had some trepidation about leaving his room. He had a sense that he didn't want to go far enough to lose sight of the hotel. Was this some derivative of Stockholm Syndrome? Had just eleven days if one counted the first day, a Sunday paralyzed his ability to go about a free man? And yet, he pushed himself further away from the hotel and into the Underground station for his second ride since being in London.

Trump, ever the evil person, began to call the virus, the China Virus, a means to instigate hatred for Asians throughout America. What an unprincipled miserable person! David used much harsher language, but his past week and a half in stir, confinement, lock-down or up, jail, call it what you will made it a game to devise more words to describe the orange bigot, scam artist, fraud, and all-purpose waste of human protoplasm.

Ok, now everyone reading this knows how Mr. Green felt about our past president, and it is doubtful that the reader even if he or she wishes will find any subtleties when it comes to speaking of the past inhabitant of the White House.

David, always the one calling for evidence, facts, cognitive engagement only, realized that he was totally warped by his own emotions about the orange buffoon. He'd read that there were Germans who felt the same way about Hitler, even making fun of his mustache, his Austrian destruction of High German and little Napoleonic self - importance. Some may have referred to a Napoleonic Complex for the little house painter and surely artists, cartoonists and people paid for the written word made mincemeat of Humpty Dumpty Trumpty as well.

Through the four years of consummate lies, half-truths, rants on Twitter, love affairs with foreign despots, authoritarian murderers and bullies, David tried desperately to equate the heinous crimes of leaders he did not find as onerous but could not. He saw what he believed to be political shenanigans perpetrated by Democrats and Republicans alike, protested as a member of a Veterans for No More Wars alongside peace loving men and women who represented various shades of the same plank.

He'd been a member since Bush 2 sent troops to Iraq to assassinate Sadam and his military. As a member of a chapter, he stood in the middle of the town square and held banners, hoisted the American flag, and accepted the middle fingers of so many who drove by in disgust with what he was doing.

Over the years he did a one-year stint as chapter president, represented his colleagues to conventions and even coordinated one held at a nearby university. Over three hundred Vets and their other halves flew, drove, took the dog bus, Greyhound, and even hitchhiked to the convention to be with their brethren and sisters against the full scaled war against the horrible

Iraqis who had weapons of mass destruction to use against the "free world". David never knew this to be true, but that was the reason given by President Bush.

At least Bush 2 and his henchman Cheney convinced the American electorate to give them 8 years to prove their lie. No weapons of mass destruction were ever found. Oh well. "We meant well." David wished that he brought telephone numbers of the Brits who were also anti-war vets who traveled overseas to be with their American counterparts. If he'd planned on remaining in Britain, he would have planned to look them up and get together.

Then the unbelievable happened. American elected its first Black president, his beautiful family and even a new hypo allergenic male Portuguese Water Dog within months of occupation of the White House. Malia and Sasha loved Bo and went to Sidwell Friends School and became young women whose mother and father were wonderful parents.

Trouble is, was, however one thinks of it, the warring nature of the American mindset continued. It didn't matter whether one was Donkey or Elephant- War is a Scam. Resources and ideology are its bedfellows and Obama and Bush pushed for both unabashedly. Most of David's friends saw no difference between the two parties. They both mourned publicly for the youth that they were responsible for killing overseas wherever they were stationed, but the thought of having a world without war was anathema.

America fell in love with the hoopla and glory of a peace time military who fought wars which were never declared by the Congress. These atrocities were simply called actions, not wars.

The Congress has yet to withdraw its permission for the President of the United States to assert Emergency Powers at his (hopefully someday her) whim. It is a disgrace and proof of our blood thirsty drive for power, resources, and ideological control of the world. Ah, but at least good readers all empires fall. We are no different.

David remembered going to Chicago with a former president of the chapter and providing security for about fifty Afghanistan and/or Iraqi vets, some ambulatory, others in wheelchairs pushed by their comrades both men and women. He and about thirty other older Vets held a thick yellow rope around the youngsters who'd decided to throw their metals into a pond around a building where generals and high government officials from the North Atlantic Treaty Organization (NATO) were meeting to declare their unity in the fight against terrorism, not their own, the others' heinous acts. They marched from the loop to McCormick Place where the NATO big Whigs were meeting.

Even Jesse Jackson and his entourage of security, media, and TV camera men couldn't break through the line. My friend at the time, a Viet Nam grunt, held them back at the instructions of the march leaders. The only one given permission to break through was a woman from Democracy Now. Green pondered her name, but it wouldn't come, and he cursed himself and his lapses of memory. He saw her in his mind's eye, her grey hair, her pinched features, and furrow above her eyes and the world on her shoulders. Maybe she was a female Atlas.

Her eyes reminded him of sad pools of murky water which seemed always to be pondering the woes of the world. What was her name? It would come later when he was on the toilet or eating an egg McMuffin somewhere. Senior moments were becoming more bothersome.

Upon arrival, each of the men and women stepped up to the moat around the conference center, read a prepared script, all bringing tears to the old guys and gals and one by one they threw their medals over the fence into the water. It was a replay of Viet Nam vets throwing theirs into the pond in front of the Lincoln Memorial so many years ago. As he wrote this saga, tears welled up in David's eyes, his heart grew heavy and then he wept.

Green thought of his dogs in Willow, Alaska and the name of his tiny kennel, Throw Away Resting Place for dogs no one wanted. How apropos and so sad. So many veterans were treated the same as his dogs.

What was that woman's name? Still nothing, but after the march tired, hot, and thirsty Ted and David fell to the grassy knoll and rested. One of the vets who we came to know was being interviewed by the talk show host and we listened to his story. It would appear all over the world in a few days and the journalist would be considered for a Pulitzer Prize.

This was the first time that a group known as ANTIFA was present at anything concerning peace, social justice, and war atrocities as far as David knew.

David had never heard of these black hooded, masked people who were there to make sure that cops and rednecks did not interfere with the solemnity of the protest. He was in the front of the march and later heard that Chicago's finest had attacked the loud, angry anti-Fascist group and one of the women he knew, a Quaker with a Friends national contingent feared these masked loud and threatening people.

David lost her willingness to forgive and forget forever when he tried vainly to explain that they were on the side of peace and social justice. Her fear of them could not be mollified. For the duration of David's life, she treated him like an enemy, and he doubted anything had changed. He tried to apologize; She wanted no part of his contrition. He wondered what sect of the Quakers she may have come from and thought perhaps it was the Nixon faction.

So many years ago and now the Trumpers hate ANTIFA and Black Lives Matter because they are terrorists as far as the breakaway, Trump faction is concerned. Perhaps this woman's fear and condemnation was but a forewarning of the movement. And in truth had there been a senior citizen arm of the group which apparently there is not, David would have joined without a doubt. He already embraced BLM and believed that Black and Brown people in America were treated atrociously by the police, White society, and every other group in authority. Power concedes nothing without demand. David found the author. It was Fredrick Douglas.

BLM and ANTIFA were making their demands known. So had the KKK, the Insurrectionists on January 6th and the Tea Party.

And now sitting in his tiny room in London, free from quarantine he thought of the heterogeneity of the people at the hotel, guests who wandered in and out, the thousands of people he saw in the plaza in front of the Underground, and he again had to question the exceptionality of the United States and Trump's Make America Great Again mantra which rang hollow to the old man.

CHAPTER 3

You got to pay to stay

Except for money spent on food at the corner grocery store, coffee, and Egg McMuffins at the McDonald's across the street and a few amenities little money had been spent, that is except for the nightly hotel room cost. After three nights the receptionist decided to give David a discount on his room for the duration of the stay in quarantine. David used credit cards mostly anyway because many Brits didn't want to handle bills touched by the hotel guests for fear of contracting Covid - 19. So different than the irresponsibility he'd encountered in Alaska. Someone said that as a Libertarian he had a right to wear a mask or not, get vaccinated or not, stand as close to anyone he wished to or not, and generally do what he wished or not. Was this a political statement or only plain stupidity or not?

He thought about continuing his trip to North Africa. Yet, he didn't want to spend his vacation in quarantine on a layover or as a final destination. At least in England, the language barrier was minimal, that is except for the surprises on 119 when he called to tell them what he was doing or get confirmation that he was not doing anything worthy of a fine or even worse, real incarceration.

Cheap-0 Air with their sales personnel sitting almost upon each other's laps in small call centers in India and parts of South America were only too happy to sell the unexpecting client tickets wherever they wished to go, and the reps could find tickets. David purchased such a ticket one way from London to Lisbon, Portugal thinking that Portugal was a haven against the virus.

Not to be. Five days before he was scheduled to fly on a Portuguese airline, he found that he would be staying overnight in Madrid and that Madrid was considered a hot spot for travelers. It could mean being deported at his expense, sleeping for ten or more hours in the airport, if they allowed him to do so, or facing ten to twelve more days of quarantine, this time in Madrid.

He called Cheap-0 but they would not refund his money because their policy is that refunds will be forthcoming if the money is asked for within 24 hours of sale. They apparently took no responsibility for anything they had no control over. So David lost the $103 to Cheap-0 Air and they lost a customer for good or so he told himself in a moment of anger. He doubted that these businessmen or women would care about a customer's complaint. Remember that David adopted the cliché about fooling one the first time and so on.

True, he was out of quarantine, but the saga was not over, far from it. There are variations on the theme. But his freedom meant that he could go anywhere he wished in London and

England and so he boarded the Underground with the intention to find the hotel he stayed in 60 some years before.

It was called the Union Jack Hotel for military from all over the British Commonwealth. They also allowed enlisted troops from allied countries to stay there and while there an unexploded bomb from WWII days was found in the Thames just below the Waterloo Bridge. David had just walked over the bridge and within feet of where the bomb was found. Within the hour bomb squads, police and emergency paramedics were on the bridge while a huge crane was summoned to remove the bomb.

Not then, when he was but a young pup in the Artillery in Germany and still wet behind the ears, but years later when he taught English in Hanoi and visited Cambodia and saw men, women, and children without limbs from unexploded ordinance from the American War in Southeast Asia, did he realize that he, too, could have been a casuality of this bomb left unexploded so near to him while staying at the Union Jack. Now close to his eighty-third birthday, he wanted to visit the hotel again and relive his memories on scene. He was 19 yrs. old, some sixty plus years ago. What a difference a few years make.

He took the Victoria Station line to Oxford Circle and then the Bakerloo train to Waterloo. Everything looked the same under the city in the Tube Underground. But Waterloo had to be right, and the Thames River would not have changed its course in just sixty some years. So he got off. Signs on the walls pointed in all directions, some to places unheard of by David, but finally he found Waterloo and followed the crowd.

Everywhere in the stations were signs to wear masks, keep one's distance from each other, fight the monster. David couldn't see one person who did not follow the government's order, except for one or two people who wore no mask, but had badges clearly seen which stated that they were exempt perhaps due to physical or mental reasons such as asthma or clinical claustrophobia.

Finding the steps and escalators, he found himself upstairs and asked a porter for directions to the Waterloo Bridge over the river Thames. Apparently, the station was a good mile or more from the bridge. The neighborhood was not busy with people scurrying here and there as it had been at his hotel, and he seemed to be surrounded by brick, red, and brown factory like buildings.

The old man asked directions of passersby Brits mentioning the hotel by name. No one seemed to know anything about the Union Jack, but one good Samaritan took pity on a lost Yank and pointed to two bridges with lorries speeding by overhead. He told David to go to the middle of the two bridges, turn right and he thought he'd find the hotel.

David's right leg throbbed, muscles begged for rest and to not be pushed to endure the damp, cold and partially rainy weather. But he plunged on to reconnect with his past. The good fellow who'd directed him was off by a block and David found himself on a road marked Alaska Street. He was amazed, excited, and curious, all at once. In all of London what a coincidence.

It was posted on the bricks of a building with graffiti below the street sign. The warehouse or store was marked

Wellington, but on closer look it turned out to be a hotel with signage about food and drink.

No one was to be seen and it appeared that the hotel had seen better days and that Alaska Street was in a seedy part of town. Or could it have been the effects of Covid-19? There was a sign by the Railroad Authority with Alaska Street on it and overhead the girders of one of the bridges. The thump, thump, thump of cars and trucks crossing overhead made David think of something from his youth when he was visiting Brooklyn and a relative who owned a factory nearby. Strange how the brain pulls skeletons from its long- term memory bank without reason. Correction. The image in his brain was similar to what he was seeing on Alaska Street.

The surprise of being on Alaska Street prompted David to take out his smart phone and take a couple pictures of his surroundings. Finally, a few steps later, a man in overalls, a gruffy beard and stooped shoulders appeared and David stopped him to ask about the whereabouts of the military hotel. "Ya, no problem lad, over a block. Ya can't miss it." David was easily fifty years his senior but was grateful that someone showed up to help. Was it a Cockney accent? David liked it.

One block away stood this mammoth structure with the words, *Union Jack Club* over the door and a British flag flowing in the stiff wind. The building had to have been twelve stories high. He didn't count them. This wasn't what he remembered at all… What the hell?

It strained David's neck muscles to look up at the British flag flying in the wind. Stairs leading up to the front door were at least twenty deep. Walking the steps was cumbersome and half-way up, the front door opened, and a young, physically fit tall man came out. He stopped, thinking that the old man may have needed help on the steps.

Turns out that he was a retired English prize fighter who'd been hit in the head once too often and had to leave the ring. He'd fought all over the world, held titles and was a trainee at the Club to become a physical fitness instructor. The workday was almost over, and he was just going home. Both powerful arms were covered by tattoos of women and art foreign to David. The old guy was impressed and thought of his two fading Tats, one on each arm. He laughed to himself. Even his sons made fun of their old man for getting tattooed. David mused, "Different strokes for different folks!" Or maybe a bit of rebellion against mom and dad and kids as well. David never let himself off the hook.

David told the champ his story; The young man did the same. "Ya mate, I punched their lights out in Japan, Thailand, South Africa, lots of places, but me brain ain't what it was and here I am. Sometimes I don't see too good, headaches, stumbling a bit. Teaching old men how to live longer."

He sighed and blushed. David thought he saw a tear on the lad's cheek. The pugilist suggested that David go in and have a look around. They parted ways with an elbow bump which was the Covid new handshake. The door would not open, but there was an electric call button which he pushed.

A voice answered and David explained who he was and wondered if he might have a look inside. The receptionist buzzed him in and told him that the old hotel on the river at Waterloo was no longer in use, might have been torn down by now but the young man couldn't be sure. At the same time about three or four men came out of the foyer and headed for the door. They were clearly in their fifties or sixties and looked as though they lived there. David saw some ribbons on a jacket.

He was not permitted to go any further than the reception area, but he peered behind the receptionist and could make out a vast hall with flags on the wall, apparently of military units and maybe others which represented the Crown's realm throughout the millennium.

Great Britain boasted that the sun never fell on the British holdings and that was true. Africa, India, Asia, South and North America, maybe more had military units everywhere, land, sea and air and was at one time owned by the Crown. These flags were reminders of this historical period and David thought about the Revolutionary and War of 1812 when Britain and its allies began to lose its grip on its Empire.

The U.S. assumed the role held by the Brits. All empires eventually fall and morph into some other form of life. David was always one for pontificating if only to himself but shuddered at what would become of America and grimaced at *Make America Great Again*, the Trump mantra. Even Biden made up his own mantra. Politicians…

The man, perhaps from Singapore or Malaysia, dressed smartly in a suit, could not leave his post, and gave the old man a card with the Union Jack Club logo on it. It belonged to the Membership Coordinator and the particulars like Sandell Street and the fact that it was a registered charity. Politely, the receptionist concluded their meeting and bade David adieu.

And that was it. No chance to see the historic site because it was more than a mile or two away, and David feared that his legs, especially the right one would collapse, and he might be accosted by panhandlers, or simply get lost. The Union Jack Hotel, now the mammoth residence for former military was what was left of a memory and a bomb that didn't explode,

CHAPTER 4

Routines in Stir Help
the Days Fly By

E very morning in lock down Green went through the same routine. Counting his money whether in pounds or dollars gave him a sense of security and something to do. Just trying to be certain that he knew the difference between pounds and pence was an undertaking. The British currency uses the metric system to differentiate between value and therefore everything was divisible by 100. So there are 100 pence to the pound and the pound come in one and two formidable bronze pieces.

Pounds come in denominations of 5, 10, 20 and 50 notes. The currency is beautiful with Queen Elizabeth's picture, Winston Churchill, and other English persons, political, royalty and famous people on them. The paper used is fine, colorful and has a see-through window which is small but beautifully done. The Brits no longer use the Euro due to BREXIT. The touch of the money felt good to David.

The pence are also reckoned by the number 100. So 100 pence equal one pound and there are one, two, five, ten, twenty and fifty pence pieces not nearly as thick or as formidable as the pound coins. David wished that he'd brought a magnifying glass with him to read the small print on each coin. The pence are kind of like the penny, nickel, dime, and quarter. The dollar reminded David of the pound sort of…

Each night before turning in, he emptied his pants pockets, pullover pouch and his jacket of all coins and anything else he'd placed in them during that day. His bedside table was strewn with coins and paper money. In the morning he placed all like bills and coins together and methodically counted them, sometimes twice. It was sort of his morning task before going across the street to MacDonald's or any other chore except for the two days that he had to test himself for Covid. He was amazed that he had so many coins considering that he hadn't gone anywhere or bought more than coffee, an Egg McMuffin or two. Both were smaller than in the States, probably something to do with the Metric System.

He'd read somewhere that prisoners in long term facilities, in other words the Big House developed routines to help them deal with their day because they knew not what craziness would erupt at any moment. They'd even count cigarettes as David did his money or bricks in their cells. Routines were comforting in a day full of surprises and even dullness. He had a sense that he understood what real prisoners endure.

For years he had to prick his finger for enough blood to place the specimen on a strip specifically treated to count the amount of sugar in his blood stream and record it on a tiny monitor. David often came within a few milliliters of guessing how much sugar was clogging up his body. His pancreas was not working properly. Some called it Islets of Langerhans and claimed Diabetes was caused by a malfunction in the Islets. David agreed but knew for him his Diabetes was caused by poor eating habits. He'd made the decision to use insulin rather than change his love of ice cream, M and Ms, and other foods with high sugar, carbs, and calories.

Then came the two insulins, one fast acting the other slower. He stuck himself with each based on the reading from his glucometer. He'd become immune to the pain caused by the needle injected into his tummy fat and there was enough of that. David hoped in vain that the insulin injection would act to reduce the tire around his gut, but it didn't work that way unfortunately. A Metformin pill together with a stomach powder to allow him to use the bathroom without pain and diarrhea completed his morning routine and he was ready to go. But where?

The rules for quarantine were sketchy in some respects. One could go out to a garden at the hotel for solo walks at night when no one was nearby. No garden existed at David's hotel, but a foyer of sorts gave him a place to sit at least six feet or meters from others with mask on and fingers crossed. He also bought food at the grocery store which is why he had so many coins and paper money.

Preferably, the inmate or whatever a quarantined individual was called could call restaurants and have food delivered to the receptionist at the hotel. In this huge building which wrapped around three corners it seemed the telephone did not work and so the receptionist would have to climb the stairs and knock on the door. David tried it once only.

On the other hand again the rules posted on a long piece of paper handed to David at Heathrow Airport in the little alcove where the stern woman sat who was the government's agent assigned to speak to the unprepared who landed in good faith in London, were unspecific about many topics. For instance, one could leave to submit the Covid test.

David's interpretation was that he could run across the street to MacDonald's, walk two blocks to a Kebab shack with excellent Lebanese lamb and chicken falafels and to a Starbuck's for their strong coffee. All of this had to be taken back to his room for consumption. The fear was that the people looking at him in the street were all spying on him and were tasked with reporting him to Boris immediately. Isn't conspiracy theory fun? What folly. No one even saw David. They had their own problems.

David knew he was being paranoid, that no one cared about him or even knew that he was a quarantined individual. Laughingly, he thought that perhaps they should have burned a huge Q on his forehead or made him wear an armband with capital letters in red saying Quarantined Beware! But this would have been reminiscent of the Nazis making the Jews wear armbands with the six-sided Star of David and the word Juden upon it. Maybe this was the next step to separate people.

David's wait for the results of his second and final (hopefully) test results came on his smart phone and when he read the word "Negative", he had a moment of elation and he couldn't explain it, but a sense of sadness as well. Even as this is being written, the author has a tear in his eye and a sense of loss. What in the world was that about?

David rushed down to the reception desk and the young Romanian was on duty. He smiled broadly and agreed to make a copy of the results on the printer in his cubicle for David so that everything was on paper and provable. The young man was from the capital of Romania, Bucharest where David years ago had spent a delightful few days in Constanza on the Black Sea. They reminisced about his homeland.

On Tuesday morning after a night of packing, repacking, worrying about the rain, wind and cold still prevailing in London, David walked out of the hotel a free man. A man who came from Egypt and treated David with enthusiastic respect was on duty. They'd spent many a night talking about the world politics, economy, and David's profound dislike of the former US president. The young Iraqi woman who signed out of the hotel and returned almost daily was the subject of interest late at night when David would sit and observe people coming and going constantly. She seemed to be an enigma, so young to be so paranoid.

Young couples would sign in and some of the girls looked to be underaged. So two rooms had to be rented for the night, but it was clearly a legal issue. It was doubtful that they were there as sister and brother. But David had no clue whether they were there for a night of passion or not. But seeing them brought back memorable moments.

There was also a man and his family who stayed for at least a week. David swore that he'd seen this man before on television and finally inquired whether he'd played professional basketball. Haltingly, the man at least 6:9 ft, tall admitted that he'd played for his country's team in the Olympics and professionally for a year or two in the United States. David rarely saw his wife and daughters, but the man came and went frequently. He was very cordial and always acknowledged David with a smile. Perhaps, not too many people paid him the respect David did.

But the topic of conversation was primarily about the young woman from Iraq. She seemed so guarded, so alone, and so vulnerable.

She refused to sign her name, preferring to use her fingerprint as a means of signing the registration data. She was almost constantly on the phone and talked in Arabic according to the hotel manager. When they talked together in front of David it was always in Arabic as well, but he told the old man that she could understand his Arabic, but that he had trouble understanding hers. Probably was like the difficulty David had when he spoke to a Highlander Scot whose brogue was impossible at least until he got used to it.

David took selfies with the Romanian and a young woman from the Dominican Republic who worked as a cleaning woman at the hotel. He took pictures of the Egyptian young man, but the Iraqi woman absolutely refused to have her picture taken. David also had a picture or two from the old woman whose late husband had been a famous British painter. David wondered how she did about finding his works of art.

And then pulling his suitcase behind him, his backpack securely on his back, a free man, slightly stooped over from the weight of the backpack, he left to continue his vacation or so he thought.

CHAPTER 5

Ageing is not for the weak of heart.

⸺⸺⸺

The day before he left not only did David Green make a trip to find his past on the Waterloo Bridge, but he also decided to do some reconnoitering and find the intercity bus to Oxford, England. He took the Underground to Victoria Station, a massive building with restaurants, stores and even pharmacies. Railway stations were gigantic malls.

The truth was that he was in search of self-catheters. He hated to admit that he was having problems with quasi-incontinence at home in Alaska. He'd been through three TURPS, two in Alaska and one in Asheville, North Carolina. According to the Mayo Clinic, "a TURP was a Transurethral resection of the prostate (TURP), a surgery used to treat urinary problems that are caused by an enlarged prostate.

An instrument called a resectoscope is inserted through the tip of a man's penis and into the tube which carries urine from the bladder (urethra). The resectoscope helps the doctor see and trim away excess prostate tissue that's blocking urine flow.

The TURP is generally considered an option for men who have moderate to severe urinary problems that haven't responded to medication. While TURP has been considered the most effective treatment for an enlarged prostate, several other, minimally invasive procedures are becoming more effective. These procedures generally cause fewer complications and have a quicker recovery period than TURP."

Long before this trip to North Africa, David faced three attempts to take care of his problems with his urology issues, but to no avail. So his urologist decided to try Botox which would hopefully quiet his prostate down and offer longer periods of calm and not having to go immediately. David laughed and said to himself, "Well in Alaska I can just stop the car, run around to the back, make sure no troopers are flying by and take a piss," He doubted realtors told old men about this.

Not so in sophisticated Florida where David would have been arrested, thrown in the slammer and probably pay a hefty fine for lewd and lascivious behavior. Dogs could get away with it, not two legged dogs.

Always a sob sister, David felt badly for women. In AK, the abbreviation for Alaska, there was always a tree(s) they could go behind or a hill to disappear, but Florida and all urban communities in the lower 48 were just as perilous for women as men. Let's celebrate equality between the sexes.

Botox worked, sort of. The prostate fell into a slumber and David went through a period of retention of urine quite unhealthy. The fear was that the kidneys would fail and that could be calamitous. Now the reader understands the need for self -administered catheters. Look what some of you youngsters have to look forward to upon reaching elderhood. David wondered whether this word elderhood even existed. If not, he thought, "Just add it to the next dictionaries if enough people are willing to use it."

Long term memory kicked in and David remembered that he and his friend Aron tried to get Webster's Dictionary Corporation to incorporate a word "Petrogal" into their lexicon. The boys had an acquaintance, who portrayed a naivety, a gullibility which was preplanned and seemed to be a deliberate manipulation of a situation.

David and Aron played with derivatives of the novel word and submitted them. They made a noun, an adjective, verb and even adverb to be used in the new dictionary. At that time, David tried to remember when it was, he must have been about fifteen or sixteen, some 20,000 people had to submit an affidavit that they would use the word, prove that they had in fact used it at least once and would continue to use it when called for. Unfortunately, his attempt at augmenting the English language went nowhere.

Green realized that he'd lost the trend of what he was talking about originally, a mind warp he called it and tried to remember what he was discussing before this business about how to get a word used in a dictionary. Oh yes, the pharmacy called Boots. They were all over England and one was at the Victoria Station.

Botox had done its job so well that the spicket was turned off altogether. The urologist gave David several self-catheters, taught him to use it or rather a young rather comely woman taught him to insert it, etc. etc. David had to struggle with having a beautiful young woman teach him to perform the feat. He asked her whether she was embarrassed, and she admitted that at first, she was, but she got over it. She blushed and turned slightly red but regained her composure.

He had an immediate flash back to his dad and Haitian woman and what she had to do for him. A moment of wistfulness and sadness wrapped together invaded David's being and he had a question pop into his head, "Is this all there is left?" He quickly dispelled it, cocked his head, and spat out, "What the hell, let's get on with life!"

Boots didn't carry catheters. The pharmacist told him that he'd have to go to a specialty shop for them. Oh, and it required a script from a doctor. David thought back to Hanoi and the pharmacy where every medication David had ever taken could be bought over the counter without having to pay some doctor to prescribe the medicine. He remembered that opioids were different, but even they were attainable with a little ingenuity. That was not David's issue, but friends told him that he could get whatever he wanted under the table. A lot of expatriates with physical and mental issues had no problem meeting their needs without going through a clinic. There was no Veterans Administration in Viet Nam at that time after the American War as the Vietnamese called it.

Botox took its time wearing off and slowly with a lot of pushing he was able to pass his urine, but not without accidents along the way.

Every back pain worried David that he may have kidney issues cropping up. The thought preoccupied him at first, but gradually dissipated.

Following tiny signs in the Victorian Station of pictures of little buses and the word coach, the word the Brits used for bus, he followed the signs and finally arrived at four or five beautiful, big double decker buses lined up on the street. They were marked London to Oxford.

Asking a driver how often the buses run and whether there was a senior discount for riding, he was gratified to find out that these buses left every half hour and that there was indeed a discount. All he would have to do is pay the driver of the bus when he got on. They ran 24/7 but only hourly at night.

The Victorian Bus Depot was catty cornered from the Oxford busses parked along the street, and David walked across the street to reconnoiter the station and what, when how much a bus to Bournemouth, England would be. He finally found the correct queue and bought a one-way ticket for Sunday. Buying the ticket over the smart phone would have been slightly cheaper, but David's skills with the phone were limited to making a phone call. He wished for a dumb phone.

He felt immensely proud of himself for negotiating his reconnoitering. He felt that the only issue was what the weather would bring tomorrow when he left and how his right leg would hold up,

CHAPTER 6

Goodbye Quarantine, Hello Oxford

He left his room wistfully, backpack on after hoisting it way above his head and experiencing it falling into place on his back. His computer was placed in two plastic bags which he'd paid for at the grocery stores where he bought sandwiches, chocolate bars, yogurt and great cookies with raisons and oatmeal in them. Not exactly the correct diet for a diabetic, but oh so good. David's mouth watered as he thought about his diet. Grocery stores were really huge buffets in a sense.

Saying goodbye to the desk clerk, another Egyptian with a broad smile but someone who David did not recognize, he negotiated the five steps to the sidewalk. The wind was brisk, but thankfully there was no rain. He was a free man, free to wander all over England, but David had not checked to see whether this applied to Scotland, Ireland, and Wales. Having never been in Wales, David gave thought to going and adding Tom Jones' home to his list of visited countries.

Next to the McDonald's was a Tube entrance. David stepped carefully around a homeless individual sleeping on a cardboard mattress and covered by a tattered coat. He turned back for another look at his hotel and sighed. He would never, never forget his stay there and a sense of overwhelming love for his room, his window, and the few people he talked with. He remembered an old man in a movie that was released from a long prison term who killed himself because he missed his friends, routines and even the "screws", the guards in the prison. He couldn't deal with being outside, a free man. David shed tears just thinking of this character in the movie.

He carried his suitcase down a long flight of steps and walked underground across the pavilion and into the Kings Cross Rail Station with the underground subway (American word for English Tube). It seemed like thousands of people were rushing here and there like a swarm of ants. He felt like one of the Brits rushing to work or wherever and headed for the Victorian train.

He was able to use his Alaskan Airline credit card because it had some sort of electronic detector which, when operational, allowed him to pass through the gates to the trains. According to a friendly service provider at the station using the card was cheaper than buying a ticket at a booth from a salesperson.

Rush hour was still going on and David waited for two or three trains before he saw a car which seemed to have room for him. He was in no hurry because he knew from his trip the day before that every half hour there would be another bus to Oxford.

David sat in the street level rather than climbing the stairs to the second story of the bus. Masks were required before the driver would leave, that is except for him. Of course, he was protected by a plastic shield surrounding his throne with all the dials, huge steering wheel and change producer for those who paid by pence and pound coins.

The trip took about two and a half hours accounting for traffic congestion and any unforeseen events. Some people got on along the way and some hopped off in small hamlets. TV screens on each deck spelled out the route, the next village, and the exact time. All David could think about was the Greyhound Bus service without any of the sophistication of this London to Oxford bus. Greyhound offered overweight drivers who treated passengers with loud, obnoxious, threatening rants. Clearly the passenger was the enemy, the driver the tin god and ruler of his or her vehicle and no passenger better forget it.

It saddened David to see what had become of the Dog bus as he liked to call it. He'd ridden the Greyhound since he was fifteen, over sixty-five years and lamented the deterioration of the company, the service, and the clientele. Even newer models soon lost their shine, spit and polish. He'd traveled in intercity buses in some fifty or more countries and none, absolutely none were as seedy as those in the "greatest country in the world." If MAGA meant anything it should be MGGA, Make Greyhound Great Again and that would mean going back to the 1950's.

An idea wouldn't leave David's brain. Not all, but many drivers seemed to use their position to bully, prove their authority, and belittle passengers on the Dog Bus, Greyhound.

Nowhere was this more evident than at the Port Authority, the huge building in downtown Manhattan where seats were uncomfortable, lines formed hours before the busses left for wherever they were going and rude, obnoxious drivers had their moments of glory at the expense of paying customers. David didn't know it then, but he would encounter this again when he returned to the U.S.

The worse part of the story was that buying a ticket from a live salesperson behind a screen was impossible. Everything had to be done by computer. David thought of senior citizens who had no computer or if they did were not savvy at buying tickets with their smart phones.

David didn't have to deal with Greyhound now. The bus pulled into Oxford, England around 12:30 in the afternoon and everyone got off refreshed and smiling. He loved the ride, the bus and appreciated the helpful driver.

He asked him where he might find a hotel and the driver suggested walking around the corner and that there would be many to choose from on Broad Street. The weather was somewhat gloomy, but no rain, a good sign. David didn't want his backpack and suitcase to get wet. He'd discovered a small tear in the lining of his suitcase where the zipper needed fixing. David feared that the zipper would malfunction, and he'd have to find rope to close his case.

So Boris Johnson and his health department decided that May 17th would be the first day that restaurants, hotels, bars, and other businesses which catered to tourists would open fully for services. David was not aware of this fact since he'd had no trouble getting into the hotel where he was quarantined in London.

First one and then another hotelier mournfully turned David away because they were not allowed to accept guests. One suggested that he go to such and such a place which David did. Up twenty or more steps lugging his suitcase, backpack digging into his shoulders. Close to exhaustion, he entered the reception area of his third or fourth inn and was met by a pretty, young girl who explained that the hotel couldn't accept guests. A middle-aged woman sitting at a computer looked over, saw the forlorn expression on David's face and took pity on him. She walked over to her worker and proclaimed that David fit an exception to the rule in that he was old, had no place to go and that the rule was that she could give him a room under those conditions. David was never so happy to fall into the category of a man destitute with nowhere to rest his head for a night. He didn't even mind being called "old".

The hotel director told him that he could stay the night but would have to find other quarters for the next night because they were booked.

He could then return for the third night because they had a room available. He took the room sight unseen with gratitude for her finding the exception to the rule which gave him a bed.

He promised to return for his third and last night in Oxford and asked for recommendations for the second night. The young woman promised to make some calls and find him a room which she did. A young strapping lad carried his suitcase up two flights of stairs to a tiny room overlooking the street and across from what appeared to be a theater closed due to Covid-19. A group of men and a couple of women sat in the doorway of the theater, appeared to live rough, that is on the street. They all seemed to share something in a paper bag, probably canned iced tea or not. People passed them and paid no heed and they in return did not harass or panhandle as far as David could see. Live and let live seemed to be the rule.

The best way to see a city when one has limited time is to take a city tour on a bus of course. Green decided that he would do so the next day, but having a roof over his head, it was time to walk about. The hotel was adjoined to a shop for tourists with merchandise made in China but with Oxford written all over the hoodies, sweatshirts, t-shirts, and caps. It turned out to be owned by the same people who owned the hotel. David looked around, but he saw nothing appealing.

Not far from the hotel was a street blocked off from automobile traffic with cafes, shops, towers, and churches built over a thousand years ago. Racking his brain to remember some of the history, Henry the Eighth, known for multiple marriages, telling the Pope to get lost and starting the Church of England so that he could divorce one woman for another always made David think about his five marriages.

Oxford University was, if not the oldest, certainly one of the oldest and most famous in the world. Even Clinton studied there when he was young. David wondered how many young English girls he'd bedded as a student and whether any of them became tour guides with titillating stories to tell. Of course, they'd have to know their audience.

He stopped for a scone and coffee at a cozy outdoor café and enjoyed his first full day of freedom from the tyranny of quarantine. Chuckling, David loved exaggerating his adventure. The ancient cobblestones were hard on his feet, but just thinking of the antiquity of these streets, the history, lore, and kings who passed on the same road he did made David feel a sense of awe and piety all at once. It is not following in the footprints but being in them and having a sense like déjà vu. He suspected that most human beings had similar experiences and maybe even contemplated what that meant.

David realized that he was low on pounds, the money that is, and asked where he might exchange some US money for English currency.

He was directed to a bank and walked there to take care of business. It was his first time in an English bank and was surprised at the politeness of the young woman who treated him as though he was the most important client she had that day.

He could have used cash in the transaction, but David wanted to see if his card would work for him. The little whatever it was called did the trick. Apparently, it triggered electronic transactions anywhere in the world and David had his pounds without any issues. He did have to show his passport. Unlike the Jews of Europe in Hitler's purge, David's passport was not stamped with the word Quarantine embossed on it. Having money created a security unlike any other and a feeling of wellness.

Seeing a bookstore on the main street where his hotel was located, he entered after looking at the book covers in the window. There were biographies of Obama, Winston Churchill, and of course the Royal family. David would have loved to see some of his books on the shelves, but there were none. He mused, "Ah, the weight of mediocrity."

One book stood out. It was called The Ratline Love, Lies and Justice on the trail of Nazi Fugitive Otto Wachter and his wife Caroline. David was initially attracted to the word

Ratline because it reminded him humorously of Rats Mouth, Florida, or Boca Raton if one speaks Spanish. David knew of Elie Wiesel, the Nazi hunter, but he had never heard of the Wachters. It intrigued his curiosity, and he purchased the book for 9.99 pounds. He figured the book to be about $15.00 roughly.

Wandering the street which was off limits to all vehicles except ambulances and police vehicles, David ran into some Evangelical Christians imploring people to stop and learn about their Lord and Savior Jesus Christ. David was stunned, He'd read that in Europe religion was a dying superstition especially among the young. But he assumed that these street preachers didn't get the word.

Two of the religious folks decided to (I almost wrote attack) speak with him and wouldn't take No for an answer. They'd been trained to ignore disinterest and pursue with vigor. A woman about 60 or so began to tell David her life story of divorce, prostitution, destitution and finally finding Jesus who has saved her life. It almost sounded like she found a second mate.

David knew many Evangelicals and realized that they operated from a different part of the brain than he did for the most part. Emotion cannot be reasoned with or deal with evidence and fact. Or so David told himself. He'd come to a compromise position which ran, "To each his/her own" These people were no different than Evangelicals back in the United States as far as he could tell.

Another woman who originally came from Southern India told him her story, how she came to know Jesus and how it changed her life. David could not find the connection but listened.

One of the men with his wife and small children was standing by and turned out to be American from Northeast Pennsylvania and knew the college which David went to after he got out of the Army. This man seemed to be a leader of the group and David and he spoke about PA. and almost everything except for religion. The young man excused himself and went over to his wife and never came back.

Funny thing about the whole episode was that the Evangelicals were hawking their message in front of a church which may have been a thousand years old and built sometime in the reign of Henry VIII. He started the Church of England so that he could divorce one of his many wives. Here in the United States the Episcopalian Church is the Church of England. David thought that many Episcopalians saw their church as the authentic Catholic Church, not the Roman Catholic or for that matter the Greek or Russian Orthodox Churches. He thought to himself that someday, he would do some research to check his facts. At the moment what he remembered needed verification.

Restaurants were still closed and would be until the next week on Monday, May 17th which meant that David would have to shop at the local grocery store and eat sandwiches, cookies, and drink orange/mango juice again.

The tiny room in the hotel provided a single bed, small table, and separate bathroom. It measured about three feet by five feet. David peered out the window and saw the same gang of partiers, laughing, cross legged on the pavement in the alcove at the theater while an occasional student or two passed by. Again there was no hassle or panhandling. Again live and let live flooded David's thoughts.

He started The Ratline novel by the barrister Philippe Sands, a well-known writer in the British Isles. David was impressed by what seemed to be a precise, almost surgical approach which Sands took to deal with a subject so morbid and tragic, the destruction of an entire people in Europe by a madman Adolph Hitler and those who accompanied him on his genocidal efforts to rid Europe of all the Jews.

Otto Wachter was a Nazi high ranking officer in the SS and general staff of the Wehrmacht. According to Sands and his fellow researchers, Wachter was responsible for the deaths of thousands of Jews he sent to the camps to be exterminated.

Meticulous research revealed many letters from Wachter's wife who bore him six children, one of whom spent his life speaking out to anyone who would listen that his father was really a kindhearted, savior of many Jews and others and deserved a medal, not a death sentence at the hands of the Americans, Russians, and other allies. Wachter dies in the book, and the question asked is whether he was assassinated by poison and by whom if so.

At times dry, perfunctory, and written in legalese like language, David read on with a sense of despair because he considered himself a Jew even if not religious, practicing or even believing in Yahweh. But David had his own sense that one could neither prove nor disprove the existence of God. Rather he believed that humanity, at least on this planet, could not be the top of the food chain, that human beings were much too imperfect to have the honor of controlling the universe.

Rather, in a light-hearted fashion, David when asked, sometimes when not, told people that he assumed that this entity called God in English, Dieu in French, Gott in German and so on came back to see what he/she had created, gagged, and said, "Did I make this mess? I can do better than this. Practice makes perfect." With that this supreme whatever took leave and went elsewhere to try again. This was all that David Green would say about this entity. As for a son, forget it… A superstitious anthropomorphic feel- good Jewish kid who may have lived, maybe not, but definitely did not like the gloom and doom of the Jewish laws and died because of it.

David learned, much from Sand's book and the work of people like Elie Wiesel and Simon Wiesenthal. For so many years many people died because they did not recognize this man Jesus as a legitimate messiah. David wondered if not accepting Trump as God's emissary to the world would cause the same destruction eventually.

David guessed that there always had to be a fall guy or a fallen people for those in the majority to destroy, or wipe out. Was it human nature or some other manifestation? Some Jews joined forces with Christians and became Messianic Jews, Jews for Jesus and other names not known by David. He'd even known Christians who were raised in Christian homes, baptized, and may have even been pastors, priests or whatever and decided to wear the Star of David while embracing the Messianic Jewish movement.

David bore them no ill will. Even as a child he'd been close to an Orthodox Jewish family who had a son who became a Messianic Jew and made his life's mission to bring people to Jesus. Even his sister and her husband migrated to Israel and raised their children as Messianic Jews. David remembered going to shul with the family during the High Holidays, where the women sat in the bleachers while the men prayed, swayed and begged God to forgive them their sins on Yom Kippur, the Day of Atonement. All this in honor of the Books of Leviticus and Deuteronomy.

Green suspected that had his friend's father been alive to see what his son had become, that alone would have driven his dad to his grave,

Yet, for David they both were far from where he was. One based his life on tradition, orthodoxy and a religion which gave all to a religion of blind faith, blind adherence to a law which did not grow with societal needs, and blind worship of a supreme being which was intolerant of any but its world view. The Ten Commandments were arbitrary in David's opinion.

The son, on the other hand, appeared to base his life on blind superstition, blind adherence to a faith devoid of cognition, and blind acceptance of a religion of unbelievable nonsense. Regardless, they both allowed blindness to rule their lives. David felt sad and wondered whether he was correct about all this. As in most of his writing, here, too he hoped that all sides would show him the error of his thinking. None had done so up to now.

The next morning David had to repack, gather his belongings, and negotiate the winding staircase to go to his next hotel that had been arranged for him by the Brazilian young woman. He thanked the hotel administrator and promised to return for the third and last night in Oxford.

The new hotel registration worker welcomed him and led David to a room even smaller than the room at the previous hotel. It appeared to be just big enough to enter, put his gear down and turn around. On the other hand the shower was great with hot water and a sink that he could shave in. David was ready to find the tourist double decker bus to see the town of Oxford.

The prices were reasonable and there was a small discount for the elderly over 65 years of age. One could get on and off at will at each of 20 stops, stay a while and hop on another bus at no cost. What amazed David was that there were multiple colleges, all apparently part of the university system known as Oxford University. The buildings were everywhere, and one was more elegant and imposing than the last.

The same can be said for churches. Old, brick buildings one with a spire which seemed to reach for the heavens, another with two or three towers doing the same. Names like Trinity College, Hertford College, and St. Catherine's College left little doubt that Oxford was a city of historical wonder and that all colleges were somehow tied to the Roman Catholic and Protestant churches. The towers were imposing as well, and David believed that some had been used as prisons a thousand years before. Earphones were given to the tourists and commentary could be listened to in fourteen languages. A great deal of history was spoken about by two voices, one a young girl, the other a youthful boy. All in all the price of the ticket was well worth the trip. David felt that he had a great introduction to the city.

He didn't get off the bus because he felt that he'd do better to stay on and see everything offered and by the time the bus had made two complete rounds of the route, David was tired and wanted to get some lunch or an early dinner and go to sleep. He was beginning to feel his age and his body was telling him, "Enough!"

Again the restaurants were not opened yet, not until May 17th by order of the high command at Number 10 Downy Street in London. So once again, off to the grocery store and two premade sandwiches, orange/mango juice and a delicious chocolate bar made for his dinner.

David thought about the double decker experience. It had been cold, windy and a few showers added to the need to go inside the bus where the wind beat upon the windowpane and seeing was hampered by the rains. But the high walls of the Oxford castle and prison-built hundreds of years before, the twenty, maybe more colleges built to withstand years of rain, wind and sandstorms, the libraries, markets, and museums all impressed David and he thought about his tiny town in the Mat-Su Borough of Alaska which he called home. Were these two total opposite spaces really in the same universe? It was difficult to reconcile and then David fell asleep and dreamt of Henry VIII. What would he have thought if he wandered upon tiny Wasilla or even smaller Willow, Alaska? One thing he had in common with some of the Willow Billies, Henry and they did have lots of wives. But David doubted that any of them were beheaded or that any of the Alaskans started a new religion in order to remarry.

The next day true to his word David packed up, left the temporary quarters, and returned to the original hotel. It was Saturday and the young woman who'd found him a night at the Empress Hotel and the even tinier broom closet of a room was off. A beautiful Romanian girl was working the weekend shift and showed him back to the same room he'd slept in the first night. And yes, the streets were empty except for the four or five souls on their cardboard mattresses, huddled together against the wind and rain sleeping under the alcove. They seemed so peaceful.

Quarantine seemed so far in the past and David wandered the streets, drank strong black coffee, and ate delicious pastry while watching the streets come alive and the young, beautiful college students studying and kibbitzing at adjacent tables. Here and there older women gave David a glance and continued walking their little dogs. All the dogs were on leash and were well behaved. David shook his head, thinking of his five dogs. They would have to go to finishing school here in Oxford if he moved them to Great Britain.

Musing to himself David wondered how Reba III, a mix between a German Shepherd and maybe a fox father, Chucky Cheese, a husky mix with a wolf from Point Hope on the Chucksi Sea near Barrow or what used to be Barrow but was now called Utqiaġvik. Brits and their dogs would probably consider David's dogs as woefully wanting.

Point Barrow was named after Sir John Barrow of the British Admiralty by explorer Frederick William Beechey in 1825. In an October 2016 referendum, city voters narrowly approved to change its name which became official on December 1. The population of Utquiagvik is nearly all Inupiat, Innuit. Why would they want a White man's name? This information again from everyman's Wikipedia.

David continued listing his four- legged children in his head. Gracie Girl, another Pt. Hope dog was found wandering as a little puppy in a garbage bin and was full of worms. David took her and after several bouts of intestinal upheaval and several other physical problems which set David back a few thousand dollars seemed to be doing well (Knock on wood). He named her for his fifth and last wife who succumbed to Congestive Heart Failure in 2017. David could never tell a half lie and often admitted to himself that she divorced him because she could not endure Alaskan weather or isolation. He, on the other hand, could not break away from his first love, the Last Frontier.

WuWu, a pot-bellied pig look alike from the fishing village of Dillingham became David's old girl when her owner and his wife showed up in Willow with seventy dogs, no money to feed them, and a vile temper on his part. Green and the dog catcher of the borough along with some dog mushers went to their house and took several of the dogs for dog teams while David inherited old WuWu, probably a great, great grandmother of some of the seventy hounds. Not long after, the husband, a veteran was thrown in jail because he beat up his wife and threatened to burn down the house. Anyway WuWu was very demanding. She didn't bark; She wu, wued.

David's last acquisition was Jjay, a Karelian Bear Dog mix. Karelians come from Finland originally from an area known as Kerelia where bears roam the tundra. They were bred to fight off the grizzlies or black bears and brought to Alaska to do the same. Jjay's personal past was unknown, but he became and still does frantic when in a moving vehicle. David had no idea what caused this terror. For the first year Jjay looked for every opportunity to bolt from his fenced yard and run off, but then made his peace with the old man and didn't try to escape at every turn.

He could have been killed because he ran across the highway at least four or five times and David would have to stop traffic on the highway and someone else would capture Jjay. He was also a humper to show David who was boss. David realized how much he missed his kids and felt a sudden urge to be with them. Laughing he realized that none of them would fit into Oxford's toleration for dog life on the streets and in the parks. They were Alaskans through and through, and would never like being controlled like these Lhasa Apsos, Westies, Yorkies, and Spaniels, or even the graceful Greyhounds retired from the world of dog racing. They seemed to prance, not walk.

One more night, repacking, counting all his money at least that which was left, he carefully closed his suitcase. He imaged it is splitting open and all his clothes dumping out on the street. The thought of it produced a sense of embarrassment mixed with fear. He didn't want anyone to see his dirty underwear.

David did some writing on his compute, checked his email and Facebook entries. He gazed out the window and took a last peek to make sure that his friends sitting in the alcove were ok and off to sleep and dreamland. He slept restlessly and woke often to relieve himself. He purposively did not take too much insulin because he didn't want to deal with a sugar low. That didn't stop excruciating muscle cramps and he had to apply some Theraworx to ease the pain. He felt his age and shed a tear of loneliness and self-pity. And then it was time to dress and leave Oxford for another adventure to Bournemouth.

CHAPTER 7

Goodbye Oxford and Memories of Youth

S unday morning, foggy, and damp but not raining or windy David departed. He had choices about which bus to take back to London. His trip to Bournemouth on the English Channel would not start until 1:30 in the afternoon and the trip to London was only a two-and-a-half-hour drive. Calculating the fact that it was Sunday and probably that meant less traffic particularly in London, but always planning for the worst- case scenario such as a breakdown, or even an accident meant that an earlier start was in order. David believed that back up plans were vital and particularly so for elders like himself. Backup plans provided for less anxiety, more control over one's life and a sense of wellbeing.

The day before David found a cap, a beautiful blue, felt like material with the word Oxford and a crest with Latin words on it and bought it. It would hang with his other twenty or more hats from around the world and be a testament to his having visited the historic city. Each hat brought back memories, probably never to be revisited. A Russian military cap with loads of insignia from the days of the USSR, a fez from Turkey, hill country ceremonial hats from Thailand, Viet Nam and Laos where David watched and participated in ceremonies, a hat or two from Dublin, Scotland and of course Australia and New Zealand adorned his wall. African indigenous hats from Lesotho, Mozambique, and Botswana, rich in color and bearing the history of their lands joined masks brought over to Alaska to be joined by Athabascan, Inuit and Aleutian head ware and masks made from the hides of wild animals.

For David, each hat and mask were not only a testament of his travels, but also had their own tales to tell. These were his history, his legacy, and his love.

Hoisting his backpack and swinging it onto his back, now with the Ratline book added was a feat. He grabbed his suitcase, one that the airlines would allow to go with the passenger to be placed in an overhead bin. Being blue with a small pocket that he placed his calling card in and a frazzled dirty yellow ribbon tied securely on to the handle so that he would be able to spot the luggage if he needed to have it placed in the hold beneath the plane. David bade goodbye to his cubicle of a room with the fine hot water shower. He wished that his shower at home was half as good. It was pitiful next to the English shower.

He negotiated slowly down a steep, winding set of steps, holding on to the wall, always afraid that his vertigo would interfere with his upright walking and he'd lose his balance.

Finally he got to the receptionist level where a new employee greeted him at the desk. She smiled, thanked him for being a guest at the hotel and asked whether someone could help him with his luggage down the narrow, long flight of steps to the ground floor. He thanked her and the same young man who'd helped him before appeared. He took the bag, and they managed the stairway with no problem. David tipped him with a two-pound coin which brought a wide smile to the lad's face. David was off for a new adventure.

It was still early and the rough living crew across the street in the alcove were asleep and made no effort to rise and say Cheerio. David smiled at his thought that he should wish them well. He walked the half mile or so to the bus station. He saw things that he'd missed coming into the city.

He passed a couple of hostels which were marked backpacker's hotels and one rundown, seedy hotel with broken windowpanes on the second or third floor. Even Oxford had its underbelly. But David had seen no backpackers while he was wandering around. Perhaps Covid-19 and the rules from the government meant that the hostels were also closed at least until May 17th when the restrictions would be lifted. The old guy shuttered wondering what he would have done had the wonderful hotelier not let him in under rule whatever. Of course, the folks in the alcove might have made room for the Yank and let him sleep with them. David pondered where did they go to urinate and defecate.

He mused thinking of the words they might have used rather than the three syllable words in his vocabulary.

No one was at the bus station when he got there, but the chairs were comfortable, and he waited for the next coach. He pulled the Ratline book from his backpack.

Each fact and piece of evidence were so meticulously laid out to convince the courts. If Otto Wachter was ever caught and brought to justice as so many former Nazis had been at Nuremberg and elsewhere, Wachter would be hanged for his atrocities during the war.

The old man had a flash back to his youth when he played with a German kid who lived a block away. His father was one of those Nazis who was spared prison time and was brought to the States to provide information on others and work for the Federal Government. Hanz was about David's age and was so sad.

David's grandma suspected that something was wrong with Hanzi and told David's mother that the child was being abused some way and the police should be called. She didn't know what was going on, but she knew something was terribly wrong. The child never smiled, was skittish around male adults and could only play with David when his father was away.

There were no Departments of Child Welfare back then, no social workers who visited homes of children suspected of being physically, sexually, or emotionally abused. Neglect, the most frequent problem for child welfare workers was not talked about openly.

Somehow the police got wind of Hanze's home life and found that the boy was kept in a closet in the basement at night. It turned out that the father, an SS colonel wanted his son to be strong, remain faithful to the Fuhrer, and be ready when Germany would rise again, if not under Hitler, then another savior. When the law arrested the father and mother for child endangerment, the father explained that he had been raised to be a soldier for the Nazi Party and he was simply doing what had been done to him. His form of discipline and child rearing seemed to be taken from the City State of Sparta in Greece. Make the child strong and warrior like by treating him with no mercy, harshly and not sparing the whip if the child rebelled. It may not have sat well with a court, and David never saw his friend again. Apparently, he was taken away from the parents and sent somewhere else to live, perhaps a juvenile home for orphans.

David wondered where Hans was now. Was he alive? Did his parents ever soften or even repent? If Hans was alive, had he become a Trumper? Had he embraced his parent's rigid adherence to a new Fuhrer? David didn't even know the family surname. He wiped a tear from his eye just as a new bus pulled up marked London. David left his valise in the bin on the main deck and climbed the stairs to get a better view of the countryside and they were off to London.

CHAPTER 8

Introduction to the Ratline and more Memories

N o accidents, no congestion, nothing impeded a fast and relaxing trip to Victoria Station not too far from Buckingham Palace. It was about 10:30 and David had three hours to wait for another bus, this time to Bournemouth on the English Channel. It is a tourist attraction particularly for Brits who love to play on the beach and surf the waves.

David could have left his luggage at the Victoria Coach Station, taken an Underground to Buckingham Palace to see the changing of the Guard and play tourist. But his leg was giving him trouble again and it would have taken him a half hour just to get to the Tube, board a train and walk up to the area. No telling how far he would have had to walk after that.

So instead he found a seat at the appropriate Queue where his bus would be waiting for passengers and pulled out a chocolate bar, had a bottle of water with him which he cracked open and devoured the entire bar. So mouthwatering yummy. Green didn't want to think about the sugar intake.

A handful of passengers gathered over the hour and a half, about three times more than on the trip between Oxford and London. Of course it was early afternoon. David pulled out his book about Nazi hunters. Sands wasn't just an attorney; He was a historian, geographer, journalist, and barrister, all wrapped in one. He'd written a book which became famous in Europe and gave him notoriety and a place within literary circles.

In one section, a note to the reader, the author discussed the name of a town which changed its name at least four or five times depending on which country occupied it and when. This changing of names was not a new phenomenon when one considered that Austria, Poland, Germany, Russia, and Ukraine played a sort of King of the Mountain game throughout Europe, first one conquering, then another and each time the names of towns would be altered by the winner of the game. For instance, New York was called New Amsterdam when the Dutch oversaw that part of the New World. When the British took over, they named the area New York.

Sands stated that Lemberg, Lviv, Lvov and Lwow (with an accent mark not found on this computer) were all the same place just not at the same time. David found this interesting because he remembered that his grandmother had told him long ago that her village changed names like diapers she said. Those were her words and David chuckled. Must have been confusing for the postal services when they had to post letters to the correct place.

David's grandmother came from the Austro-Hungarian Empire to the United States after the beginning of the 20th Century, but she could not be sure of the name of her village. She, like millions of Europeans, came through Ellis Island and sometimes the immigration officers who sat at the desks checking personal papers of the new arrivals changed names, birth countries and towns so that they could make sense of it all.

Often these uniformed men were from Ireland, Scotland and other parts of Western Europe and had little patience for Eastern Europeans. If the men wore yarmulka's, had long names, their names were changed to short ones and often names unheard of in their tiny villages and ghettos from which they came. "You're in America now Laddy; Become American or else!" Most of the time it was said with a twinkle in the guard's eye, but not always.

The most critical issue was to check for anyone with a disease such as cholera, influenza-any disease that could be spread and possibly cause a pandemic. If one or more refugees came off a boat ill, they were quarantined and David lamented, "just like I was, but I was never sick from the mass murderer Covid-19."

Sands, the author of Ratline never directly said it, but implied that his grandparents were Jews rounded up in the village by Wachter and sent to the camps for extermination. David assumed that along with Simon Wiesenthal and other Nazi hunters, Sands who focused on Otto Wachter specifically also would be considered a Nazi hunter.

Reading the book was tedious due to the difficulty of following all the characters, particularly the Nazi's family which included his wife who wrote thousands of letters to her husband and others in an attempt to tell the world that her husband was a good and kind man, not a butcher as so many people believed. She wanted desperately to see him pardoned and exonerated from any of the "lies" about him.

David outlined passages from the book which he hoped one day to do research on to further his understanding of the Nazi's consummate hatred of the Jews and their determination to wipe all Jews off the face of the Earth. If anything, this book was a proof against those who would deny that there had been a holocaust or that six million had perished. But Nay Sayers have no interest in truth, evidence, or facts. They are consumed by hatred of Jews, and it is an emotional, not cognitive hatred.

By the same token David could find nothing in the book about the killing of many other groups such as gypsies, intellectually challenged individuals and many more groups the Nazis wished to exterminate as though they were vermin. This included homosexuals, but that was tricky because some high- ranking Nazis were also closet gays, a word that did not become synonymous with homosexuals or lesbians until the 1960's.

Sands goes on in the book to explain the concept of the Ratline as a means which war criminals like Wachter used to escape the allies' retribution by going to friendly Vatican priests and others in Rome who would arrange passage to Argentina where Peron had sympathy for the former Nazi leadership and would offer sanctuary. Another indisputable fact was that after the war, the American Government was so intent on destroying Communism that they allowed certain high- ranking Nazis to come to America to work for various agencies. Those Nazis literally got away with murder, genocide, and destruction of millions of people and the United States government was complicit, all in the name of saving the freedom loving Democracies from Communism.

David found that as he read memories of his own interfered with the reading. For instance, he remembered Catholic boys surrounding him at the playground, calling him Christ killer, and Jew Boy. Some would try to take his pants down to see what they had been taught at home or by the priests at their churches, that Jews cut off part of a Jewish baby's penis. They didn't know that circumcision was a religious rite and that it was just the foreskin that was removed, not the penis itself.

Shaking his head, sighing, and letting a breath of air flow from his lips, David realized that had it not been for Abraham at the ripe old age of ninety-nine who was ostensibly commanded by the All Mighty to circumcise himself and all the males over the age of thirteen, many Jewish boys bullied by Catholic and other ignorant Protestants might have been spared the indignities of having their pants pulled down to see what it was all about. David's mom, something of a pacifist, told David to just turn the other cheek and forgive their ignorance. He wasn't built that way. David had a thought. Could this Abraham have really done this to himself? Even drinking to oblivion would not be enough for pain relief.

David could not turn the other cheek as his mother wished him to do, so he compromised with his mother's wishes by simply holding the culprits and whispering in their ears, "Relax, it is wrong to do what you want to do."

Not until Basic Training at Ft. Jackson, South Carolina when he was just nineteen years old did, he really renounce his mom's words and beat the hell out of three boys from Georgia or Florida, he couldn't remember which. He thought back to the incident.

It was an eight-man wall tent with double decker cots, just like in summer camp. One night three poorly educated boys who'd been taught by their pastors that Jews had tails and horns decided that they wanted to see David's tail and feel his horns on his head. They planned to grab him, pull his shorts down and look for themselves.

The dorm guard made his rounds; It was about 2 am. And then the rural bumpkins made their way past the potbellied stove red hot from the coals. February in South Carolina could provide freezing weather. The three boys about David's age crept across the tent dirt floor and pulled David from his bed.

David's bunk was on the bottom and his friend from North Carolina, Joe awoke and the two destroyed David's curious attackers. Joe pulled the red hot poker from the stove and began to brand one of the boys while David launched his body into the other two. Hearing the commotion, the tent leader a young boy who had a year of college under his belt jumped down from his bed and called everyone to attention. The watch on duty just outside rushed in, turned on the light and confronted everyone with a stern. "Cut this fuckin' shit out." It was over and the boys hurting and befuddled crept back to their beds.

David thanked his bunk pal profusely, turned away and smiled.

"Sorry Mom. Never again, I won't start anything, but I will finish it with all my strength I have". The young private was proud of himself and couldn't help being confused. Joe was from the South too, but different than the three dumb asses. Why?

In the morning the drill sergeant, a Puerto Rican with years of service arrived around 4 am and in words which can only be described as over the top woke everyone. He'd been briefed by the duty guard and asked David if he wanted to prefer charges against the three, one of whom had a burn on his arm from the poker. David declined the offer. Sgt. What was his name? David cursed his memory lapse. The furious drill sergeant told the three how lucky they were and that anything more from them and they'd be court marshalled and would spend their Army days in a place called Leavenworth. The boys hung their heads and had to apologize or else which they did halfheartedly. But David had no more trouble from them and more importantly during a three- day holiday, Joe, his bunk buddy invited David to Asheville, North Carolina to meet his parents and his girl.

David mused, "and they never got to see my tail or feel my horns on my head." He laughed aloud in the Victorian Coach Station and people looked at him and chalked it up to an old gent talking to himself which wasn't exactly wrong.

There were no interstates yet, so the Greyhound trip to the mountains took forever over bumpy roads and hilly countryside through the night. Little did David realize that visiting Northwestern North Carolina would eventually be a pivotal piece of his history in the future and that he would live there in a commune with elders like himself.

Columbia, South Carolina, and Ft. Jackson named for Andrew Jackson, seventh president of the country and a general before launching his political life is still home to basic training but has no wall tents for its soldiers. The basic trainees have hotel like suites compared to 1958 and David's experiences. Gung ho grunts like to say that was the real Army and some had crude names for the current Army recruits. But then David had to admit that the old timers who fought in Korea or even some really old duds who fought in WWII belittled the new guys. It was a game. He imagined that it was still going on now and would for eternity.

David went to Artillery School to learn to kill people from afar while his friend went on to Ft. Gordon to be a military policeman. They never saw each other again, but David tried to find him and when he moved to Asheville years later, he went over to the Veterans Administration hospital and asked whether they knew of a Joey Thompson. They were reluctant to answer, but one assistant let on that that name was not on their patient roster.

It was time for passengers to get on the bus for the seashore town of Bournemouth. David closed his Ratline book and got on the coach.

CHAPTER 9

David's Glance Back

———————

The bus ride to Bournemouth was pleasant without rain and David gazed out his window at rows of homes joined together in typical British fashion with chimneys, some belching twirling, curlicue white smoke. Many homes had small plots which were cordoned off with small gardens with colorful flowers and perhaps some vegetables. In some ways these neighborhoods reminded him of urban living in America.

Kids rode their bicycles and here and there a couple enjoyed their Sunday afternoon jogging or walking hand in hand. It seemed that everyone except the children wore masks. Brits took this monster seriously. Whether it was because they were afraid of being fined if they did not wear protection or because they, too, were willing to endure the coverings for the greater good of all, he did not know. But, thinking of the major resistance in parts of the US and the hue and cry of Libertarians who equated the wearing of masks with denying them their rights to do as they wished without regards for others made

David cringe. Some of their language was strong, vulgar, and threatening. This was not the first time he criticized these people. Many of the same people thought of themselves as good Christians following in the footsteps of their lord and savior. David could only shake his head in confusion.

He thought back to the beginning of this getaway from mountains of snow and temps in the 30's and even colder in the mornings. He left, it seemed like ages ago, but it was only two or three weeks, took an Alaskan Airline plane to Seattle and another directly to Ft. Lauderdale, Hollywood's busy terminals. He was going to see his family.

Always mostly unspoken but never far from the surface was discomfort in dealing with his son who he believed still harbored major resentment against him for having left his mother. "I want to play golf on Sunday, so maybe you should consider leaving on Saturday." Not very polite, but to the point. He was saying, "I can only deal with you for so long."

That gave David two days in Florida to see the family. Both grandchildren were home from their respective colleges and his oldest grandson lived up in Boynton Beach with his girlfriend. So the only one he would not see was his older son near Niagara Falls in Northern New York. David planned to go through Buffalo on his way home to Alaska to see him.

David developed a tough skin over the years and never forgot that he left his sons' mother. He'd take what was offered and move on that Saturday. Trite as it was the old man developed a philosophy of take what you can get. And besides, he had a loving relationship with his grandkids, and he'd spend time with them. He also loved his son's wife, but she was a nurse at a hospital, and he doubted she'd be at home.

The hospitals were crying for nurses thanks to Covid, and she rarely said, "No".

So David used some of his frequent flyer miles on American Airlines and got a ticket from Florida to London, one way. The goal was to spend a day or two in London and then on to North Africa. He never even thought that he might have to be detained. Who would have known? Every day the latest information was posted and changed.

David saw nothing about quarantine. Besides, he was already vaccinated and tested without any signs of the dreaded killer.

For three or four weeks while still in Alaska, David considered cutting his hair and beard. He hadn't been to a barbershop in nearly a year and looked like a hermit who lived deep within the Bush.

A friend of his son's, a young man from Tasmania who'd immigrated to Florida with his family took David to his barbershop and within twenty minutes the floor was cluttered with grey hair and matted curls. The metamorphosis was amazing. He barely recognized himself in the mirror. His family said that he looked years younger. David wasn't so sure that he wanted to look younger.

The next day, in compliance with American Airlines, David went to an urgent care facility and got the first of many tests to prove that he did not have Covid-19. It was quick and expensive, but the clinic billed Medicare for the procedure. It was a test which could be run through a lab quickly and within a half hour, David had a letter signed electronically by a physician stating that he was negative. The clinic had over a hundred dollars for their two minutes of work. The letter stated that these results were good for 48 hours. The octogenarian wondered whether a new industry was on the horizon. Ah yes, Capitalism at work.

On Friday night, he took his son, daughter-in-law, his three grandchildren and a girlfriend of one of the grandkids to an Indian restaurant and they feasted on excellent spicy Indian cuisine. David's mouth watered just thinking of the great food. Florida's governor had decreed that businesses, including restaurants, were to open to the public. Such a difference in the way the British government dealt with this disease and the governor of Florida did. He seemed to allow politics and economics to interfere with the science of this disease.

David remembered that after dinner back at the house, his son turned on the TV to watch some sport's event. In an intermission, he told David about a miniseries called Queen's Gambit that he thought David would love. David loved chess, bemoaned the fact that he would never be anything more than a mediocre pawn pusher at best, but spent many days and nights wishing he were.

David played chess on his smart phone and probably lost half of his games. Sometimes, he seemed to be better and won and was congratulated by a little man lodged within his smart phone. He vowed that when he returned, he would sign up with Netflix and watch the series. David calculated that he might have spent thousands of hours playing the game of kings.

He'd known some great masters who made their living playing the game and now with the Queen's Gambit, queens as well. One of his opponents was the half- brother of the man accused of killing JFK. He was a tech sergeant in the Air Force and on the base chess club with David. After the assassination, the sergeant could only go home, to work, his parttime job and David's house to play chess. He was hounded by the FBI for information about his family and any contacts with his brother and cautioned not to discuss the murder with anyone. So that subject was taboo. The two played chess and talked about little else.

There was more to the story. David, a first lieutenant was on temporary duty and stopped in Dallas at an all -night diner for breakfast off Interstate 35. It was back in 1964, summer and hotter than hell. A beautiful blond in a fur coat came into the diner. She looked scared, actually terrified.

David mused at the use of the word "hell." He always asked people who used the word whether it was cold or hot down there? It all depended on who one asked. David figured it was just a manmade gimmick to keep people on the straight and narrow. He'd read that some people assumed it was hot as Hades; Others shivered at the thought of it. For them it was colder than they'd ever experienced or wanted to.

Anyway, a beautiful young woman appeared and seeing David and another Lieutenant may have thought these were safe, so she asked if she could sit with them. It turned out she was a stripper who worked for Jack Ruby at his club, the guy who killed Oswald on TV. She blurted out that the killing of Kennedy was by the crime bosses, and they paid Oswald to do it. They were pals with Ruby. It was a major conspiracy. Then she bolted from the table and ran out of the diner without eating her breakfast that the military men paid for.

David couldn't be sure, but a couple of months later he read that a body had been discovered in a culvert off a highway near

Dallas. The body belonged to a young blond who worked for Jack Ruby, the killer of Oswalt who ostensibly killed JFK. Was she the same woman who didn't eat her breakfast? David never got an answer to that question.

Finally, the bus arrived at its terminal in Bournemouth, and it began to rain. David could smell the sea air and see seagulls flying everywhere. They seemed to be on a mission.

He got off the bus and asked for possible hotels he might stay in for a couple of nights. Someone suggested a hotel in the middle of the town and suggested it was at least four kilometers away. David took a taxi into the town square area to the hotel.

CHAPTER 10

Staying in the Lap of History

ournemouth is not pronounced Bornmouth. The "mouth" is pronounced like Vermouth and the "Bourne" is pronounced like the last name of Jason Bourne, the spy who lost his memory. David chuckled to himself because he could identify with losing one's memory. Lots of movies have been made about Jason Bourne and appear on television routinely. David could only wish that he'd had even one appearance or reference on TV. He figured he would die someday in anonymity.

About the Vermouth, he drank no alcoholic beverage, probably because of his Diabetes. He preferred ice cream as his killer rather than booze.

David never heard of this seaside resort town on the English Channel across from France, but the ticket agent at the Victorian Bus Station recommended it because she'd been there numerous times with her family as a little girl. It was a favorite of Londoners.

A couple young people on the bus had their surf boards with them. The boards were a lot longer than David thought they would be.

The taxi driver drove David to a hotel, the Prince or something like it. Carrying his backpack in his left hand and the suitcase by its handle in his right, he climbed three or four steps and entered. There were no people in the reception area and the hotel seemed disserted.

David had a déjà vu like experience or as Yogi Berra used to say, "déjà vu all over again." A man probably in his fifties, portly, balding with a Sears and Roebuck like suit and tie appeared and frowned.

"Sir, we are closed until May 17th by order of the Health Department. You shouldn't have come in." He gave David a stern look.

David knew of the mandate until the next day and started to tell him that the health department left room for allowing someone with either health issues not related to Covid or someone who might be indigent or have other special needs to be given a room. This the old man learned in Oxford from the concierge at the hotel where he stayed. He loved her flexibility.

"But, I am nearly 83 years old, have Diabetes and leg muscle cramping. Don't your regulations state that under extreme circumstances you can waive your rules and allow me to stay for a night?"

The man straightened up and reiterated that his hotel was closed, and he would not bend the rules. David had a moment of stress and fear intertwined. Again David tried to persuade the gentleman to reconsider, but he would not budge. "I am sorry but there are no rooms here. You must leave immediately."

"Well do you have any recommendations elsewhere, any hotels which might let an old man spend the night?" The man thought for a moment and suggested a couple of other hotels assuming that David knew them and where they were. The man came around from his desk and summarily escorted David to the door. Not a good beginning to a short respite in Bournemouth.

He found himself on the sidewalk and wondering whether he'd have to find an alcove to bed down in for one night. Not since he was a young backpacker wandering the world had he had to sleep rough. At his age, it did not sound appealing or even possible.

David had no idea where the hotels were that the stickler for following rules had suggested he try. Turning left he saw a huge, old hotel with a sign Royal Bath. On the sign beneath the name was Britannia Hotels and an artist's picture of a Christian king or prince who held a scepter in his right hand and sat on what appeared to be a throne.

He walked the slight elevation to the hotel, went in fearing the worse and again a man appeared from a back office. He was refined, and at the same time very friendly and after David cried on his shoulder so to speak smiled, and assigned him Room 235, a small broom closet of sorts, but David was thankful to have a bed, shower and in such a beautiful, old, elegant, and charming hotel.

A young girl from Greece with a beautiful accent came in and the Lebanese man explained that she was there to be interviewed for a position to begin tomorrow when once again the hotel would be opened for business, and they expected a full house. David, if he liked the room, sight unseen could remain for the three days he hoped to be in Bournemouth.

The room was through two doors, sort of hidden from the rest of the floor, kind of an afterthought. There was a brochure on the little table that stated that Royal Bath was over two hundred years old and built in the time of Queen Victoria who reigned for over 60 years. It was said that she was beloved by the entire world, but David wondered whether indigenous people in Africa, Asia, Australia, and New Zealand felt the same way.

David could barely open his suitcase and there was no room for him to place his computer so that he could work on a memoire of his quarantine days and his worrying about being destitute, without a bed to lie his head down and a sink to brush his teeth. It did not matter; He had a room with a window looking out on the square. To the left he could see the English Channel about a good block away. The old man sighed and was at peace. Rain clouds seemed to be moving in and the wind picked up. He fell asleep for about a half hour, rose and left the room.

He took the stairs rather than the elevator and wandered around the hotel. The restaurants, gift shop and workout room were locked down at least until everything reopened. But the beautiful abundant sitting room was open and could be used so long as people sat with masks on and about 6 meters from one another.

It was spacious, charming in an old European décor with paintings on the wall, flowers in large vases and one could imagine that in its day kings and queens may have sat comfortably and who knows Winnie may have also spent time smoking cigars and reading his newspaper.

Outside was a garden with paths to stroll in and benches to sit when desired. This was old Europe, not the 21st Century high tech, fast paced England of today. David sat in an old high back beautifully upholstered chair and was swept away to the days of Victoria, Queen of the British Isles. No one bothered him and he remained in his chair for an hour or more, sometimes napping, mostly luxuriating in the past.

Realizing that it was already late and that darkness would soon descend upon Bournemouth, he decided to take a walk. To the left down a path of maybe a block or two was the channel, to the right and across the street, the hotel he wasn't permitted to sleep in and further along a street to stores and the center of the city.

Sunday night stores that were opened like the grocery stores closed early as was their routine even without Covid. David found the town grocery and managed to get in just before closing time. He bought two readymade sandwiches, one tuna on dark bread, the other a chicken salad also on dark bread. He found a bottle of orange/mango juice same brand as in London and Oxford and for sweets some raison, oats cookies. The bill came to around nine or ten pounds. He never bothered to change pounds into dollars in his head for fear that he may have paid a lot of money for his dinner. It would have been the same had they continued to use Euros. He still would not have tried to figure out the value in US currency. It didn't matter really. He still needed to eat, and restaurants were not opened.

People strolled along the road which below it one could see a beautiful park with a path which possibly he could have taken to get back to his hotel, but David remained on the road he had used to get to the center lest he got lost. On the street were buses marked to little villages, some quite a few kilometers from Bournemouth.

David went back to the Royal Bath Hotel and to the huge sitting room. He sat next to a small table to eat his dinner, devoured his sandwiches, drank his orange/mango juice, and ate a cookie or two. His first royal dinner in the hotel of kings and queens was delicious, if even not fit for royalty.

That first night he sat in a chair of nobility and grandeur and felt a sense of abundant satisfaction. He looked at a little stage with a piano on it and imagined concerts which may have been given for the guests with quartets from around the Isles and mainland Europe playing beautiful classical music for their listening pleasure.

David's memory kicked in and he remembered having the same sense of wellbeing in Hanoi, Viet Nam at his favorite bar and restaurant, the R&R Club on La Sur.

Every Thursday night, a quartet from the Vietnamese Symphony would play for two or three hours for the people who loved classical music. Even the rowdy crowd of Deadheads and Rock and Roll patrons would mellow out and listen to two violins, a viola and a cellist play exquisite music. For those few hours once a week, the R&R Club became a musical salon of rich, soulful music heard in the great halls of symphonic glory.

Around 8:30 pm he began to nod off, cleaned his area and took the lift to the third floor and his little broom closet. He crept into bed after taking his insulin, medications and listened to rain upon the windowpane. He slept blissfully without any horrible muscle cramps.

CHAPTER 11

Are the Lilliputs related to Lilliputians

‾‾‾‾‾‾‾

Monday morning was a pivotal day for England. Boris Johnson, the Prime Minister, who himself had contracted Covid-19 and had inaugurated BREXIT in England and opened businesses like restaurants, hotels, face to face meetings and other events to his people.

The looming question was always present. Would this move precipitate a rise in Covid cases? Would everything done on May 17th have to be retracted? English health officials needed to be vigilant.

David awoke to a cold, breezy day and determined that he was going to the beach, not to swim, but to walk to the pier, watch surfers brave the waters in their waterproof suits to ride the waves.

He no longer had to fear that some government official would swoop down on him and throw him into quarantine again for sleeping in a public facility. He felt for the second time, the first being the end of quarantine in London, that he was totally free to be himself and roam wherever he pleased, sleep wherever he could afford to do so, eat in, rather than take out, a restaurant and love life as he did before Covid.

The walk to the beach was on a path with beautiful flowers in gardens, down a winding road and voila, the white sands and rolling waters with their high waves. It was early in the morning about seven or eight and already he could make out surfers lying on their boards, arms pumping, heading out to meet their waves. One and then another rose, balanced him or herself with arms flung out and road the surf. Each fell or jumped clear of their boards into the freezing waters, gathered their boards and went back for more. They were not gluttons for punishment, but rather adventure and the promise of the "big one". These were hardy Brits and others, adventure junkies and worshippers of living on the edge.

It is said that Bournemouth is not as much of a surfer's delight as some of the beaches in Hawaii, but it seemed that those here loved it. David walked out on the pier almost to the end, saw more lithe, beautiful people rise over the banks, walk on the white sandy beautiful beach, and descend into the water. Several of the athletes were young women, the age of his granddaughter and he thought to himself how much life they had left to live and play. He also noticed that the rubber suits or whatever the fabric was accentuated their fine figures and he felt something within himself akin to arousal. He laughed at himself.

As he walked back on the pier toward the beach, he ran into two middle aged workmen and began a conversation with them. One was a veteran and recognized David's cap which showed that he, too, was a vet. David asked whether this town had been attacked during the war. "Me parents and the old folks used to say that they'd hear the planes overhead and that up the beach there were antiaircraft guns manned by the Civilian Reserve." His eyes told of horror and those family members and others who never came home.

His buddy listened intently to his friend. "My grandma, she was a spunky ol girl used to stand on the sand out there," and he pointed his finger, "and shout at the Huns. She had some words for them alright." His friend laughed and spit on the boardwalk. Both of the guys looked longingly out to where the planes flew over the Channel. Richie, that was the older one's name blurted out venomous words through clenched cigarette held lips, "Oh they had stories alright, some are still alive about your age, I'd say. When they get together in the pub, drink too much, you know, their eyes tear up remembering their friends and what happened. I wasn't even a gleam in my ol man's eye yet, but I remember hearing the stories alright,"

Apparently, Bournemouth was not targeted by the Luftwaffe, but sometimes they'd strafe the cement blocks with the guns inside them.

He didn't know much more but said that some of the men from here died fighting the Huns. David wasn't sure which war he was talking about, the first world war or the second one. They parted ways with handshakes and an admonition from the veteran, "Be careful Yank." It was good advice.

Coffee seemed like a good idea because David was chilled from the exposure to the waters, the air which was out and out cold and a desire to be able to go into a coffee shop and sit down for the first time in a long time. David couldn't even remember. He found a shop up on a hill overlooking the beach, went in and had a black, medium roast, Arabic coffee, and a peach scone. He wondered, could life be any better than this?

The shop was crowded with people and although they could have sipped their teas or coffee outside before, they crowded into the shop to sit inside, something that they hadn't been able to do for a long, long time.

David began to plan his day. Bournemouth had one of those get on, get off wherever you like and back on another bus. These tourist buses were just like the one in Oxford and David would get one. While he was talking to the two workers, he asked about a cliff partially obscured by the clouds that he saw from the beach. They told him that a bus had service to the area and that people lived out there. David wanted to go and see for himself.

He meandered his way back to his hotel and went in. Already life in the old hotel was beginning to blossom. The registration desk had a line of three or four couples, children and one or two had little dogs either in their hands or on leach.

Shops in the hotel were not opened, but they would be later in the day. They'd been closed for months as was the restaurant and bar.

Tonight the restaurant would celebrate a grand opening with opulent dining. David planned to give it a try when he returned from his tour of the island and its sights.

He took the lift up to his floor to get a windbreaker, check his cameras for their battery service and off to find city sightseeing in Bournemouth, Poole Quay and Sandbanks.

He already had the brochure about the bus trip, had read it thoroughly and was excited to get started.

The tour promised 23 bus stops, translation into 14 or more languages with the use of earphones. David didn't make use of the earphones in Oxford. He didn't want to repeat this error again, so he made sure that the first thing he did was plug in the earpieces properly.

David was given hearing aids by the VA. They discovered that he lost enough hearing while on active duty with the artillery unit in Germany but would not give him more percentage of disability or money per month for it. He often laughed about it. The government would not give him an extra hundred or even two a month but spent trillions of dollars to expand our empire all over the world and send our young men and women to every corner of the world to keep indigenous peoples "in their place."

He remembered Major General Smedley Butler, Congressional Medal of Honor recipient, Marine Corps for over thirty years who wrote the pamphlet "War is a Racket."

The general said that he spent all those years protecting big business from indigenous people who were being used, abused, and cheated by American companies. This was all in the twenties and thirties of the last century.

David belonged to a group of peacenik veterans, most of whom were combat veterans from the Korean, Viet Nam, Afghanistan, Iraqi, Kuwait and so many more conflicts that our boys and girls were sent to deal with. Oil, other resources, and accumulation of land was what these young people were protecting, not democracy or freedom in the United States.

It was a sham just like what Butler wrote about so long ago. Nothing changes, just the day and the weather.

David wondered how he got started on all of this. "Oh yes, my hearing aids. I still hear noises in my head over here too. This Tinnitus never goes away." The VA denied him 10% on this too. "So is it greedy to ask for a pittance compared to the amount taxpayers are giving for keeping our empire all over the world?" He decided to leave this question to the reader to answer.

David found the tourist bus, got on and paid a discounted fee for being a senior citizen and they were off to see Bournemouth, Lilliput, Poole, and the rest of Bournemouth not in the center of the town.

He assumed that Lilliput had some relationship to Jonathan swift's Gulliver's Travels which apparently it did not. However, he heard the speaker on his headphones speak about Baden Powell who founded the International Scouting Movement. He was born in Lilliput.

After the tourist bus experience, David went to his favorite encyclopedia, Wikipedia and found some interesting information about Swift, so all was not lost. Swift died of syphilis at the age of 35. He claimed that he got the disease from dirty bedsheets in hotels while traveling. Interesting bits of trivia fascinated David and he made note of it for future use.

He also wondered whether the description of the Lilliputians in the seminal satire Gu ll iv er's T ravels had an unspoken reference to the people of Lilliput or was the tiny village on the seacoast even founded when Swift wrote. Knowing that libel could be involved here, David decided to make it clear that there is no known reference to ancestors and that Swift had no knowledge back in his day of the people of Lilliput. David wiped his brow now that this legal question was put to rest.

Regardless, David couldn't forget the thought. He researched the origins of the tiny village that he went through on the tourist coach and found circuitous remarks about Gulliver, Swift and a famous satire in the material on the small village of Lilliput. He couldn't fit the pieces together in his head, but obviously he wasn't the first to ask questions.

The Lilliputians were tiny men who were "imbued with pretention and self- importance of full-sized men". According to the Seafarer Word Press, these tiny beings "are mean and nasty, vicious, morally corrupt, hypocritical and deceitful, jealous and envious, filled with greed and ingratitude- they are in fact fully human."

David shook his head and thought to himself that Swift must have had a crystal ball and saw the 21st Century in the United States and the entire world. Clearly, the satire was describing the horrendous and corrupt people who stroked the insurrection of January 6th, fought the current president on every attempt to heal the social, political, and economic wounds in the nation and allowed vanity and hedonism to prevail. But, in all his reading, he could find nothing to connect Lilliput and the Lilliputians.

The rest of the bus tour was peaceful and uneventful. Clearly there were many fine homes that could be seen which backed up to the beaches. Some even seemed to have beachfront private homes. The bus made a complete loop to the Sandbanks, Poole and views of Brown Sea Island and then back to Bournemouth proper. It was a very restful and peaceful ride. Again Green didn't get off of the bus to poke around in any of the villages they passed, but he could have done so and taken another bus back to the city. The sea air was delightful and made David a bit sleepy.

Returning to the hotel, he found many more people there. Most were elderly couples perhaps from London or even the French Coast. It had been so long since they were able to leave their homes, have the freedom of travel and they, too, could not wait for May 17th. Of course the hotel concierge and the pretty girls behind the desk were elated that business seemed to be returning quickly.

David went into the sitting room and many of the chairs were taken. A waiter brought drinks to the occupants and talk was lively. The kids, probably grandchildren, were having a ball chatting and laughing while the older folks spoke in quieter tones.

David met a woman who seemed to be either a widow or single from Manchester who'd had business to attend to in London and took a coach down to spend a few days at the Baths. She was a businesswoman, a real estate broker and apparently secure in her lifestyle. David told her about his grandson who was about to take a job after finishing a master's degree in real estate analysis. Commercial properties were his interest, not homes and apartments. He hoped to work in Florida so that he could be near his girlfriend who was about to start Law School. They chatted for an hour and then she excused herself.

David realized that he hadn't eaten a meal all day and thought about the opening of the hotel restaurant, but decided he'd rather walk up to the grocery store like he did the day before and be able to choose what he wanted to eat. Apparently, the menu in the hotel was limited and set due to just reopening.

He walked past the very hotel where he had been denied a bed for a night and silently thanked the balding overweight man because had he accepted David's crying on his shoulder, the Yank would never have stayed in the much more famous, elegant and historic Royal Bath, a Britannia Hotel. It was another example in his life of the yin and yang of life.

Two sandwiches, one orange/mango juice and a small, sweet peach pie and his feast was devoured back in his tiny cupboard of a room. He fell asleep after eating his gourmet meal and only awoke around midnight to undress, brush his teeth, take his insulin, and go to bed. The next day he would leave Bournemouth for London and then where?

CHAPTER 12

Covid is the "Decider" of the 21st Century.

W here to go was totally depended upon Covid. Covid ruled the world and still does. Governments, health organizations, businesses, education departments, economies, transportation, politics, and all the rest of us were and are prisoners of this pandemic.

Each day presents new messages of hope and despair super imposed upon each other. David thought about the politics of this disease and its effect ever present and totally dominating. Covid seems to have a life of its own. It is not just a disease that destroys people's lives, but also leaves a trail of tears wherever it strikes and an uncertain future for those who have had it and fear in the hearts of those who have not. He spoke aloud to himself. "Except for those fools who listen to religious zealots, politicians making points with Trumpers. What idiots!"

He was back at the hotel now, fed up with trying to figure out where he could go and not be imprisoned in a hotel or worse awaiting a government's release from their form of quarantine. Thankfully, he had the money to take care of his basic needs: food, water, shelter, and unforeseen needs that might arise. But he heard tales in England about Americans and others who had to beg their Embassy personnel for loans or outright gifts to cover their unexpected expenses. Especially some young backpackers found themselves in this predicament. David wondered if any of the people sleeping in doorways or alcoves were foreigners or for that matter from Alaska.

And then his thoughts returned to the coach ride back to London from Bournemouth. In his usual fashion of toughing it, octogenarian style, he decided to take a city bus to the coach station from which he had come three days ago. He'd taken a taxi to the hotel and the balding man who denied him a bed to sleep in for a night. David, too, was overweight and cursed his tire that surrounded his stomach.

He had a moment of regret that he thought of the balding man as fat. Maybe that was simply projection. He spent his life wondering why he thought this or that? It wasn't self-doubt exactly. It was an example of his introspection process and again whenever he felt badly that he judged people, he ended the thought pattern with, "I am who I am." What was it that a famous philosopher said, "I think therefore I am."? He reluctantly liked the statement, "Judge not lest ye be judged." He didn't trust religious proverbs generally, but this one he laughed at because he judged people routinely and knew that they judged him. He chalked it up to living.

"Someone French, but who the hell was it? Another bout of brain freeze just like a computer. He figured he'd remember sooner or later, and he could always look it up in Wikipedia. The problem was, it would consume him until he did. While on the tiny commode, David yelled out to no one, "Descartes, Cognito, ergo sum. Where the hell do I come up with these thoughts?"

He knew that the French for the Latin was, je pense, donc je suis.

"Ya, that's it I think therefore I am."

He smiled his all-knowing smug way. "Once in a while, I ain't so dumb for an old geezer".

David trudged up a long hill which winded him and caught a bus to the coach station. The cost was a seventh of the cost by taxi. He had the money, but there was a sense of pride which accompanied controlling his expenses. Some would call it cheapness; Others would smile and remember their time of bullheadedness. The bus dropped him at the station, and he bought a ticket to London. He sat for an hour at most and thought about Lilliput. Was the town simply named for Swift's satirical book and the horrible Lilliputians who tied up Gulliver? If so, whoever named it didn't think much of the citizens there. More importantly, Swift probably never equated the Lilliputians with the citizens of Lilliput.

The trip to London's Victoria Coach Depot was uneventful, but when the coach closed in on London traffic, everything seemed to slow down, and the driver arrived around two in the afternoon.

Of most importance to David was that he wanted to visit at least one country he'd never been to, and he needed to get to his computer to see which country was allowing people to enter without quarantining them immediately as had been done to him.

A Portuguese airline had a flight from London directly to Lisbon. When David called the airline, he was told that he needed a test showing that he was negative for Covid-19 within 72 hours of the time he was to fly. The test had to be a SARS-CoV-2(COVID-19) RT-PCR SWAB Fit to fly Certificate. No other test would suffice. It couldn't be a quick result test or a self- administered test. It had to be both nasal and throat tested. In some sense the test was exactly the same one which he had to self-administer when he was quarantined.

Those two tests, the second and eighth day were administered by himself, but this airline needed it done by a professional and a government approved laboratory. "Oh, one more thing it must be done within 72 hours of your flight." The airline representative repeated herself for emphasis.

The same airline had a flight to Lisbon with a layover of ten hours in Madrid, Spain. This ticket was at least $200 cheaper than the direct flight. But there were no assurances that he would not be quarantined in Madrid even though he was only passing through the country, David didn't trust that were he to try to leave the airport, he would not receive the same treatment he had in London.

Upon reaching the Victorian Coach Depot, the question became where to stay, how to find a company or laboratory to have the test taken and for it to be within the 72-hour range. David's first instinct was to go to the Underground and directly back to the hotel where he spent his quarantine. He realized that he missed the MacDonald's, the receptionists at the hotel and his room, 104. He didn't quite understand his attachment to his jail cell. Maybe the Stockholm Syndrome. Then he realized that he'd already thought of the syndrome before and shook his head at his forgetfulness.

Instead, the old guy gathered up his backpack, slung it over his head and felt it land snugly on his back and began to walk up the road away from the bus station and away from the Tube. He had no idea why he took this road, where he was going and what he would do, but it felt right.

Hotels were opened to all guests who could pay for the rooms and the first place he saw was a Best Western. He saw a sign that the hotel could arrange for a traveler's Covid test and in the foyer was a woman, the wife of the manager of the hotel. They were Lebanese and he rented a room for a night. The woman assured David that she would take care of everything for a price to get him the correct test and that she, herself, would administer it.

David had the sense that there was something not quite right about her doing the test, charging for it and at the same time having to pay over $120 for the test. The Best Western had three or four converted row houses which they'd remodeled into rooms of assorted sizes and charged accordingly by the size of the room. His was as tiny as most of the rooms he stayed in at Oxford and Bournemouth. He asked directions to restaurants, stores, and a pharmacy in the vicinity of the Best Western.

David asked for a room with a fridge to keep his insulin cool. They assigned him a room with no cold storage area and begrudgedly, a sallow faced assistant assigned him a different room which was slightly larger than the first. The wife of the manager gave David a stern look. Maybe she thought David might be looking for company and she disapproved.

After he was in the room for a short rest, he took a long walk to explore the area. He had no intention of paying the woman to administer the test at a cost and his first inclination was to look for a pharmacy which administered the test.

His flight was on Saturday, May 22nd, one day before his 83rd birthday and it was imperative that he calculate exactly when he needed to take the test and hope, actually pray which David staunchly rejected at all costs that he would not be positive. He also decided that he would purchase a ticket to the United States from the airport in Lisbon and stay in the airport as long as it takes so that he would not fall into the quarantine trap. It all depended on a negative test result.

The restaurants, bars and coffee shops in the Victorian area were plentiful and David stopped for coffee and a scone. He found a restaurant that claimed to have the best fish and chips in London and had haddock fish and chips with a strong-smelling dip for the fish and chips. It was good, but he preferred the fish and sweet potato chips in Alaska at Sheep Creek Lodge in the Talkeetna area north of his home. He'd made friends with the waitresses and together with a bowl of the best clam chowder in all of America, a large glass of root beer and six huge chunks of fish with sweet potato fries, he never left hungry. His mouth always watered, ala Pavlov's dog experiment thinking of the fish and chips at the huge log cabin restaurant with the wonderful staff.

His favorite waitress was astounding. She'd run the Iditarod, wrote beautiful prose, was a mountain climber and hurtled buildings like Wonder Woman. David laughed at this last reference. His other favorite waitress was great too. He kept running into her at the grocery store. She was a natural beauty.

"Ah, to be young again and virile, but I guess I'll just have to be content with a smile, great waitressing, and scrumptious food."

And then he spotted a pharmacy with a big sign advertising Covid-19 tests for travelers. He went in and talked to a pharmacy technician, and she assured him that with careful calculations when he was traveling, the pharmacist would give him the test at the right moment, send it to the lab and the results would be mailed to him on his smart phone and they would get a copy of the results which would be put into a formal letter to be shown at the airport to the airline representative.

David liked the assurances given him and decided there and then that he would use the pharmacy for the test and that he would not stay for more than the night he'd paid for at the Best Western London near the Victorian Station.

He went back to the little room measured in meters rather than feet which made it smaller using the metric system and fell asleep. The window in the room looked out to an alley with nothing but rubbish bins to look at.

Rainy, gloomy skies and wind greeted David as he left his room the next morning. Coffee and some sort of food was on his mind. He was in count down mode and wanted to be sure that nothing went wrong in his preparation to leave England and go to Lisbon.

David called the airline that would take him to the U.S. He used his computer to find a cheaper flight to New York from Portugal. He would stay in the airport for however long it took to go home. Cheap-O Air indicated that the cheapest flight from Lisbon was on the Portuguese airline and would leave approximately four and a half hours after landing in Lisbon from Heathrow.

He booked the flight after calculating that his test, assuming that it was negative, would fit snugly into the 72- hour time frame and he wouldn't be caught in any bind. Everything hinged on a negative test within the allotted time frame.

Then he had a thought. Certain people were exempted from all these costs and detailed calculations. He'd seen it when he arrived in London before his quarantine. These people were essential workers, military passengers, both American and others, people who had diplomatic papers, businessmen and women who somehow were also exempted and others who David could not place in categories but were free to travel without quarantine. He asked himself how it was that the Covid virus knew that these people were safe and others like himself were not. Was it all a scam of some sort? Was this just another means to bilk people out of money? And even if he were right, how could he ever prove that he was part of a governmental heist, an international conspiracy against the common man?

Later after David was home and settled with his dogs and his life, he reviewed a bank statement and realized that he spent $170.00 for the test at the pharmacy. He had no idea how much he'd spent on these Covid tests. Was it all a racket? Were the naysayers, right? Lots of questions, no answers.

David needed to return to Best Western London and get out of there. On his way back after breakfast, he found a small hotel only two blocks from his chain hotel and inquired about a room for a night. He went in and negotiated a price with a young man who sat behind a plastic shield so he wouldn't contract the horrendous disease. This hotel represented itself as a bed and breakfast, but the breakfast was a scone, coffee, and some jam according to the young man, not really a proper breakfast served to guests.

David wanted out of the Best Western, away from the business of the test being administered by the wife of the hotel administrator. So he took the room which turned out to be an afterthought in the bed and breakfast which was not really a bed and breakfast. If all went according to plan, he'd be there one night only, have his test at the pharmacy, a letter to prove he was negative and then he could go back to his room across from the train station and be off the next day to Heathrow, Lisbon and home. David had it down to an orderly and precise exit from his ordeal in London...He yearned for his little house in rural Alaska, his five four legged children and the end of his so-called vacation.

CHAPTER 13

Final Moments in London

aving ordered and paid for his two trips on the computer, one to Lisbon, the other to JFK in New York, he almost prayed that he would receive the good news that he was negative and that he'd get the results of his test on time. Cheap-O wasn't about to reimburse for the tickets. He laughed, "Maybe that's why they call themselves cheap."

On Wednesday he reported to the pharmacy on Warwick Way at his appointed time, was introduced to a beautiful woman who was the pharmacist who would stick the cotton swab in his mouth and up his nose. She was very polite, answered the few questions that David posed and assured him that everything would go like clockwork (his words, not hers). She was actually gentler than he had been on himself when he thought he might have penetrated his brain stem during quarantine. She promised to notify him on his smart phone as soon as they received the results from the laboratory. He paid the fee, his fourth in less than three weeks and thanked her for not invading the archaic part of his brain for which he received a beautiful smile and chuckle.

The chemist shop was named after the second part of a famous musical group, but David doubted that there was any relationship between the chemist shop and the famous brothers who entertained the world with their music.

The next morning, the morning that David would begin his 72- hour time frame for flying both to Lisbon and the United States, he received the promised message on his Android smart phone. Scientific jargon covered the message, but the second page contained the following:

> To Whom it may concern,
>
> We can confirm that the above-named patient had a COVID-19 RT-PCR throat and nasal swab test at our centre. (The Brits used "re" rather than "er"). May have derived from the French and was changed by those unruly revolutionaries in our colonies. That's the way David's mind worked. He read on. The result of this test was **NEGATIVE** for a current COVID-19 infection. Based on this result, the patient is currently fit to travel.

David went to the young man at the desk at his quasi bed and breakfast and asked whether he could make a copy for him on his printer and the young man agreed to do so. He was Pakistani and had a sister living in the U.S. He wanted desperately to see his sister and so David gave him his card and invited him to come up to Alaska. With letter in hand and the name of the lab in the letterhead, David had his documentation and could go back to his hotel room where he was quarantined for one more night in London.

He went over to the pharmacy and thanked them again for taking care that he received the letter promptly. They probably had nothing to do with the letter, but he wanted them to let the beautiful, blond, voluptuous woman who didn't pierce his brain stem know that all was well. For some reason, his dad's admonition came to mind which he told David so many years ago. "You can look, but you can't touch."

David assumed that this sage advice had something to do with marriage and looking but not touching another woman than one's wife. But at 82, almost 83 as though the year made a difference, David applied the cautionary remarks to age, not state of marital bliss. Dad really loved his mother, and that wasn't always easy. David shook his head and for the zillionth time thought how lucky he was that his stepfather decided to adopt him.

Green looked at his letter again and saw that it was signed by a senior biologist with a Middle Eastern name. His first name was Sadakat and David wondered if it meant charity. The Hebrew was Sadaka or something like it and he remembered that he brought his money every Sunday for charity to be given to the poor or sent to the new State of Israel born when he was ten years old. He vaguely remembered bringing money to plant trees in the new country and that the Jews were attacked by many Mid -Eastern countries which wanted to drive them into the Mediterranean Sea. There were many such wars and yet Israel prevailed.

Yes, over the years there'd been changes, many wars, thousands of Israelis, Palestinians, Arabs, Iranians, elders, children and middle- aged people dead and maimed due to war, terrorism, Israeli treatment of Palestinians and vice versa, the way that the Nazis treated the Jews during the world war and so much more.

When David visited Israel all he felt was sadness, saw so many elders with demeanors of fear, anger, and a sense of foreboding. The only happiness seemed to be among the young Sabras, those born in the Jewish State. Yet, they were brash, full of themselves it seemed and almost all the youngsters that David spoke to hated the Palestinians. Almost everyone knew someone or lost a loved one who'd died in a war with Palestinians or countries surrounding the tiny State of Israel.

David saw the same hatred in the faces of the Palestinians toward the Israelis, and he couldn't count the number of times he doubted a happy resolve of their problems with each another. Jews and Muslims were supposed to have shared the same ancestral father, Abraham but had different mothers, so theoretically they were all half brothers and sisters. They gave a whole new meaning to Family Feud.

If it hadn't been for Jewish peace groups which were dedicated to finding a mechanism of peace between the people of the tiny state of Israel and the Palestinians, David would have said that there was no hope, that the end was the destruction of everyone without consideration of what religious, political or cultural group they espoused. David believed that attacks were not only geopolitical but anti- Semitic as well. But he also believed that Israel was not treating the Palestinians fairly and that matters were growing worse, not better. In bitterness, he asked over and over again, "Where is the United Nations in this horrendous war between the Jews and Palestinians? Why has there not been a UN military force to stop the battles."

One answer lay in the make-up of the Security Council and the fact that all five of the permanent members of the Council had to agree before any military undertaking could be attempted. The Americans were often the stumbling block to intervention. Tragic! It may have been useful after WWII when the United Nations was founded, but Green doubted that the rule served the world now. No one country should stop the UN from sending a peace keeping force anywhere it was needed.

He also felt that world Jewry played a significant role in America's support of Israel and that American Jews, particularly Orthodox and Conservative elements had too much say over American foreign policy especially in Israel's favor. Add to that many Christian denominations sided with Israel against the Palestinians and lastly Palestinians were used as pawn by the rest of the Middle East to be a stone in Israel's shoes. Bad all around with little hope of a peaceful settlement.

He worried that Israel had become just like the Nazis in some way and that there were factions within the Israeli population who would be happy if the Arabs were wiped out or at least not on Israeli soil.

David knew he was no Nome Chumpsky. "No, no, not Chumpsky, Chomsky, but for the life of me I can't remember his first name." He also knew that he was no maven in the Veterans For Peace and Social Justice movement either. He couldn't remember the name of the guy who had it in for him for so many years. Just thinking of this guy brought sorrow to

David and he remembered being ostracized by him on missions to foreign countries to stand up for the oppressed and beaten down. VFP spokespersons vilified Israel and seemed to find Palestine the David in a war between David and Goliath.

There were authoritarians on the Left as well as the Right. He'd read that by a woman who explored authoritarianism and suggested that people who had to be the boss could be on all sides of the political aisle. "Oh well, that was then, and this is now." David would have loved to be considered a sage speaker, writer, and a wise person, but he was fairly sure that just as he was a mediocre chess player, he probably was so-so as a thinker as well. The thing he had going for him was that he was still upright, inquisitive, and could tie his own shoes. "Oh wait, I have Velcro." He laughed at himself. He was surprisingly good at laughing and not taking himself too seriously.

David walked back to his bed and breakfast, past a block or more long garden. A sign said it was the Victorian Garden Park and David stopped to take pictures of beautiful purple and red flowers. He'd never seen such beautiful flowers in his life. His brain seemed to explode with glee when he looked at the incredible beauty of the garden.

When he returned, he talked to the young man from Pakistan and asked him to make another copy of his test. He didn't want to take a chance that he'd lose his proof of being negative for at least 72 hours. He placed the results in a pocket of his backpack and the copy in his pants pocket just in case.

David called the hotel where he'd watched the world go by and luckily Valentine from Romania answered the phone. He was happy to talk to David, wanted to know what he'd been doing since his quarantine. He looked at his guest book to see if there would be a room for David for the night. His old room, 104 was vacant and David asked for it immediately. He wanted to stay a night, not as a captive, but a free man in his old room with a splendid view of the huge train, Tube station. He promised to tell the young man all about Oxford and Bournemouth when he got to the hotel.

With plane tickets secured, tests successfully taken and negative results in hand, David left the Bed and Breakfast on Belgrave Road in Victoria, London and walked to the Tube Station. He was getting closer to seeing his children and he admitted to himself that he missed them more than he thought he would. Chucky Cheese, Gracie Girl, Reba III, WuWu and Jjay would see their dad soon if all went as planned.

He didn't need to ask anyone directions back to the Kings Cross area of London. He was now an old timer on the Tube and knew how to find his way with help by an attendant at times. He wanted to see the hotel and people who worked there and treated him like a model prisoner. He laughed at the thought of being a model prisoner.

Rush hour was over, and he found a seat easily on the Tube. People paid him no heed and he enjoyed his anonymity as just another Londoner. Thirty-five minutes on the Tube, David marking off the stops: Green Park, Oxford Circle, Warren Street, Euston and then Kings Cross Pancras where he got off, passed his credit card over the exit light, and proceeded to the East stairwell, grabbed the handle on his suitcase and walked up a long flight of stairs to sunlight and throngs of people going and coming. The stairwell was empty now. The man on the cardboard mattress was gone, but not the mattress. No one walked on it, and it was left for its owner for the coming evening.

David experienced a sense of exhilaration as he negotiated the three or four steps to the hotel. Valentine was there and they bumped elbows, the new Covid greeting. The young Santa Dominican girl was there and she, too, was delighted to see the old man back. He'd left her a hefty tip when he departed after his quarantine. or maybe she was just genuinely happy to see the American. Her ebony skin was almost translucent. She was as beautiful as the pharmacist who'd stuck a swab up his nose and into the depths of his throat, only twenty or thirty years younger.

David had no explanation for a feeling, a sense that he was sort of home, not in Alaska, but home, nonetheless. He walked up the two short flights of stairs and opened his door. Nothing seemed to have changed except that the two single beds were made, the bathroom sparkled, and the little fridge had two fresh bottled waters in it. The window was the same, dirty glass with two panes of what looked to be cellophane, but ten clear, but still dirty glass looking out over the exchange and over to the hulking train station with the mammoth castle to the left of the station.

He had this strange feeling that he'd returned to his cell, but it didn't feel like an imprisonment, but rather something from his past. He threw his shoes off and lay down on his bed. It felt the same and he slept for about an hour. He didn't realize that he'd done a fair amount of walking, carrying his backpack and suitcase, and walking up and down stairs, although in the Tube there were escalators which seemed to go on forever.

He had another of his crazy thoughts. There used to be a man who was called Mr. Science who said that stairs were just dead escalators. "Now where the hell did that come from? Damn out of thin air I come up with these memories."

The Red Coats were gone. He imagined that they'd met in the early morning across the street near the market. He wanted to research the red coats. "The Red Coats are coming; the Red Coats are coming. Oh yes Paul Revere". But these red coats were not soldiers. They appeared to be tourists or some sort of senior citizen group who met every day when he was locked up. They seemed to gather in front of the station and then they disappeared. David never saw them leave, go into the train station or anything else. They were there and then they were gone. All wore long red coats and some of the ladies wore hats. Maybe the gentlemen did too. David couldn't remember.

He took out his laptop, placed it on the small table which held his coins when he counted them, the computer and a couple of books. He almost forgot his book Ratline. He couldn't remember whether he'd read any of it in Bournemouth. He opened all the pockets on his backpack, found the book and three or four magazines which he'd brought with him from home to read on the trip.

He'd thrown in a copy of Church &State, The New Republic, and The Nation. Some of the people in Willow, Alaska who'd been in his house called them Commie Crap. They read Gun magazines, Evangelical tracts, and whatever information they could find on Donald Trump. They were magazines for real men, but they were good natured about it, at least when in David's house.

To read or not to read, was the question David asked himself. With only twenty-four hours left before he'd get on a plane for Lisbon, he decided to go to a restaurant for a late lunch and if still hungry go over to the Kebab hole in the wall for dinner.

He also wanted to go back across the street and sit and observe the people who came out of the station or were waiting to go in. He thought back to one of the rare times that he took a chance and crossed the road to sit outside and luxuriate free from cell block 104. There were a bunch of kids, boys and girls dressed in their school clothes, not uniforms as such but girls in skirts, boys with shirts outside pants and ties probably with the school colors. David couldn't be sure.

They giggled, poked fun at each other and generally had a rousing enjoyable time. On a whim, David approached them and asked if he might ask a question of them. He explained that he was a Yank, an American which his accent gave away. They were good natured, not fearful that a pathetic old man, a pervert at that, might be trying to kidnap them for filthy sex or whatever.

So David taking the cue that he could ask them a couple of questions, went ahead. "So what do you think of Donald Trump and Brexit, and Boris Johnson?"

A young girl of maybe fifteen, sixteen tops, stuck her finger down her throat and gagged. She was an artist, had a year longer of school and hated all three Johnson, Trump and BREXIT. She was verbal, forthright, and demonstrative.

Her friends, three boys and two or three other girls were not nearly as upset as she but made it clear that they were not fans of the two political leaders but fudged their answers about the new English paradigm.

David asked whether their parents or guardians talked to them about politics and contemporary life. Some said yes; Some said no. The old man thanked them and that was that. David didn't see much difference from what he would expect from American teens and English ones. "Kids are kids; I guess they have other things on their mind."

David returned to the hotel and Valentine was just about to go home. David gave him a card with his phone number and email address and invited him to bring his wife and child to Alaska, hopefully in March to see the beginning of the Iditarod Dog Race which he hoped would get back to its usual race once Covid was over. The old man and Romanian elbow bumped, and his Egyptian friend assumed duties for the night at the hotel.

David and the young man talked for a couple of hours and David asked about the 23 yr. old Iraqi girl who kept coming back and was so guarded. She seemed to trust Memo, the only way that David could pronounce the Egyptian name without slaughtering the pronunciation totally. The girl spoke Arabic as did the Egyptian, but perhaps the closest comparison could be American English versus Scottish Highlander English. They had trouble understanding each other but remembered that he'd already written about this in his notes.

Memo told David that he believed that she was perhaps mentally ill or that at the least she was very, very strange. He decided not to carry on discussions with her because she could be nice one moment and rude and distrustful the next. So he cut off communications. He hadn't seen her for the last three or four days.

David asked about Ana, the elderly woman whose husband had been the artist and died. She did not return after she went home, a place called Brighten, England. Oh well, nothing ventured, nothing gained was all he could think of to say to himself.

It was getting late; It was time to take one last walk around the block and say goodbye to London. Tomorrow he would fly to Lisbon, Portugal and hang out for four and a half hours in the airport.

Sorrowfully, he thought about his goal to go to Morocco and other North African countries. Another time perhaps without Covid.

CHAPTER 14

Welcome to Lisbon Airport

This time it was a really goodbye or a so long, it's been good to know ya moment. The Tube train to Heathrow Airport was not difficult to find. The Underground went all the way to the airport and stopped at the majority of the terminals. David's was Terminal Two.

He received his ticket to Lisboa as the Portuguese call it. David had a window seat, and he was happy to have it because most of the scenery from 35,000 feet was beautiful. The plane flew over the English Channel into France and maybe over the Basque lands both in France and then into Spanish airspace. Mountains, rivers and what appeared to be steep valleys could be seen because the weather was perfect for viewing.

The flight took about two and a half hours in all and by about 3pm a huge city appeared, and David was fascinated to see what appeared to be a gigantic statue of Jesus of Nazareth overlooking a beautiful harbor and a bridge which was a great deal longer than the Golden Gate Bridge.

It seemed to go on and on and on. From the air it looked fairly new. The Vasco da Gama Bridge is the longest bridge in Europe. It measures over 10 miles (17 km) long and connects the northern and southern parts of Portugal. The bridge was inaugurated for the 1998 Lisbon World Exposition, and is so long that on cloudy days, it is impossible to see the other side. David checked Wikipediae for his information and was surprised to find that the Lake Pontchartrain Causeway in Louisiana was over twice the size of the bridge in Lisboa. He copied the information from Wikipedia into this information as a comparison of the two bridges. David reflected upon this information and smiled thinking that the Exceptionalists would be so happy to know that they had a bridge longer than any bridge in Europe. At least when it came to bridges, America was number one.

The Lake Pontchartrain Causeway sometimes known only as The Causeway, is a fixed link composed of two parallel bridges crossing Lake Pontchartrain in southern Louisiana, United States. The longer of the two bridges is 23.83 miles (38.35 km) long. David figured that few people knew this information.

Upon landing in the capital of Portugal, David presented his passport, showed the officer behind the plastic shield his letter showing that he was negative for Covid and was given permission to continue on to his next plane. But that was not what David wanted to do. He wanted to go into the public area of the airport to examine the stores, buy some trinkets for his friends and perhaps eat something Portuguese in a restaurant.

Snafu is snafu everywhere in the world. A uniformed woman took his passport, his letter stating that he did not have COVID and went to the back of the queues to an officer, apparently a supervisor, and talked to him. It took at least fifteen minutes but finally she came back and in surprisingly good English told David to follow her.

Fear grabbed David because this was what happened in London when he arrived. A sinking feeling that he would be quarantined again, God knows where, overwhelmed him. He began to feel pain in his chest.

The officer behind the supervisor's shield examined the passport again, looked at the letter, looked at the old man, turned to his aide, nodded, and gave him David's passport. The aide using his metal stamp stamped the passport and David sighed a relief when told by the original officer he could examine the airport before his flight to the United States. David thanked the three officers, gathered up his backpack which had been examined by a gloved officer and proceeded through a series of doors into a beautiful busy huge space filled with shops, restaurants, comfortable chairs and most importantly freedom to roam, explore and buy whatever he could afford to purchase. He thoroughly enjoyed himself. No surprise, the pain in his chest ceased almost immediately.

In London when David received his boarding passes for the two flights, the airline employee suggested that David's suitcase was too big to go in the overhead bin on the plane. She told him that he would have to allow her to send it to holding, and they would place it below the plane with other luggage. He removed some insulin and whatever he thought he might need for the flights, shoved the Diabetic materials into his backpack and hoped that he would retrieve his suitcase in New York without losing it. Of course if it got lost, the Portuguese airline would be responsible for finding it, sending it all the way to Anchorage and then Willow by some company which would deliver it to his tiny house.

But that was a gamble which meant that in Portugal he would not have to lug it around with him wherever he might go. It was a trade -off and they did not charge him for extra luggage.

He noticed that practically all of the tourist shops carried cork items. There were cork caps, purses, pins, change holders, lamp shades, and a host of other gifts. Portugal is known for its cork. For David, cork represented something one pushes into a wine bottle and that was all he knew. Again he vowed to go to his all- purpose, everyone's encyclopedia to see what it had to say about cork and Portugal's attachment to it.

He had his computer wrapped in the two plastic bags he'd had to buy at the grocery stores in England and turned it on, watched it go through its iterations indicating that it was working and finally he plugged into Wikipedia. He typed the words cork and Portugal into this find section and found the following, but not in the all- encompassing Wikipedia.

"Portugal is a major cork-grower; in fact, nearly one-third of the total cork oak area, estimated at 2,150,000 hectares (5.3 million acres) is in Portugal, which produces approximately half the cork harvested annually in the world (about 310,000 tons)" David copied more information, probably more than most people would ever wish to know, but that was his nature, Good to the last byte.

"Portugal is the world's leading cork producer, accounting for over 60% of the volume of world exports, and it has an area of cork oak corresponding to 25% of the area that exists worldwide. So when traveling across the country, especially in the Alentejo, notice how the cork oak is one of the most common trees in the landscape."

David also read that cork oak doesn't burn in a fire. His first thought when he read this information was that he wished that these trees grew in Alaska. He thought about the McKinley and Sockeye fires in his area and the horrendous amount of loss of forest, private property and the devastation upon hundreds of people who lost everything they owned. He wondered if it were possible to grow cork trees but realized that the climate might not be conducive in the Last Frontier.

He found cork fabric, rings, bags, watches, bicycles, and unimaginable cork paper, all for sale in the various shops he visited. For the right price, the shopkeepers were able to bag, box and creatively prepare the items for travel on aircraft. David found a cork cap which he bought to go with his cap and hat collection at home. Then he bought six or seven items to give to friends and family.

When he looked at his watch, he'd already spent two-thirds of his time before take-off to JFK. Lastly, he went to a restaurant and ordered something he could not pronounce to eat, a tea he didn't recognize and a desert that he should never have eaten. He was feeling elated and satiated and a bit naughty.

The electronic board showed that the flight was on time, but no gate had been assigned for boarding. English and Portuguese were the languages of choice and in fact in all countries, almost 78 or 79, but who's counting English was at least one of the languages always used to inform travelers what they wanted to know. He was told to look again for the gate in a half hour.

David saw a bookstore filled with people and he mused to himself that he never met a bookstore that he didn't like. He laughed out loud which, of course, brought stares from other travelers. He winked at a pretty elderly woman about his age. She blushed slightly and turned away.

He was, of course, thinking of the line from the thirties spoken by Will Rogers, the everyman's philosopher who was reported to say that he never met a man that he didn't like. Some people sneered at that idea, but it stuck in David's brain like glue. Strange this long-term memory. He heard that computers had short- and long-term memory and he remembered the word, "RAM" but he couldn't remember what it stood for or which it was, long or short term.

For some reason he couldn't figure out, he thought of Bill Marr, the TV talk show host and some of his solo commentaries and his rules. What did Marr have to do with Rogers? Breaking his train of thought he returned to the Big Board and found that the gate had been assigned. His right leg was achy again and this always meant that David had to limp and reduce his speed considerably. As a matter of principle, he refused to ride to the gate on a chauffeur driven little four-wheeler.

He proceeded to the gate and saw that the lines were forming for the flight to New York and John F. Kennedy Airport in Jamaica. Eight hours from takeoff, he would land in the U.S. He wondered whether they would question him about his trip, threaten quarantine and whether his son would want him to come to Buffalo to see him before David returned to Alaska.

He had an aisle seat in the middle of the plane and a half empty flight. He assumed that Covid was responsible for the few travelers. Most of the flight was crossing the Atlantic at night and there was little if anything to see until they crossed into Canadian airspace. David slept some and watched a movie someone else was watching in front of him in the middle seat. No sound, but David supplied the gist of the movie anyway.

It looked interesting. No sound, but lots of animation on the part of the actors. Apparently, a Jewish refugee made pickles and the entire film was a silent screen about the pickle maker, another man, lots of interaction in what appeared to be the streets of New York or some other big city. David could have asked for earphones for himself and watched the film, but he didn't. He checked the marque on his own screen, found the pickle maker and learned that the film was called An *American Pickle*. He decided that he would find the movie on Netflix when he returned to his home in Willow.

He has yet to watch it. But he found that this man immigrated from a small village in Lithuania or Poland, was a Jew and got a job in a pickle factory. One day he fell into a vat of pickles with brine in it. The brine apparently saved his body from deteriorating for 100 years and after being in the huge cauldron for so long, he awoke in the 21st Century and resumed his life.

David still had not seen the movie but decided that even had he seen it through he would not ruin it for anyone else who wished to watch it. And then he fell asleep and slept fitfully until the flight attendants woke him for dinner. He had no idea what time it was but calculated somewhere within an eight-hour difference between Lisbon and NYC. He ate sparingly and accepted a glass of Portuguese wine which he tasted and swished around in his mouth. Of course now science talks about freezing people until what killed them can be rectified.

Before he'd been diagnosed with Diabetes, he'd enjoyed a glass of Mateus wine from Portugal every now and then. That's what was served by the attendants and after years of not drinking any alcohol, he tried it and liked it.

After dinner or whatever meal it was considering that looking out a window everything was pitch black and he had lost complete contact with time or sense of the hour, he went to the bathroom in the rear of the plane. Negotiating the space which seemed smaller than American Airline bathrooms, he finally was able to urinate without soiling himself, a problem which he was acutely aware was becoming more problematic as he aged. He cursed his girth, his small penis and laughed at himself. Luckily, his laughter was drowned out by the engines of the plane.

When he returned the pickle guy was talking to some woman and they seemed to be involved. He had to see this movie someday, He fell asleep.

The next thing he knew the flight attendants were walking the aisles serving coffee, tea, some Danish and croissants. He asked a middle- aged attendant how much longer they had and was told that they would be landing in about two and a half hours. David fiddled with his screen, pulled up the flight plan, saw his plane over what appeared to be lights below the jet and water surrounding the lights. They were over Newfoundland or maybe Nova Scotia. It was a guess.

And then the plane veered left or south moving ever closer to New York and David's call to his son to see if he were going to get to see him.

Landing skillfully the pilots maneuvered the flying tube to a gate at the airport named for a president. The other airport was named for a famous mayor of the city of New York.

David went through the immigration process in the American citizen line, was not asked about Covid and didn't have to produce his test results. A young man smartly dressed in an Immigrations uniform asked him some perfunctory questions about what he was bringing into the country, checked his passport and said, "welcome home."

His suitcase was one of the last ones which careened down the chute and almost landed at the feet of an old woman who must have been in the front of the plane. David did not recognize her. He saw the bright, but dirty yellow ribbon, managed to scoop it off the conveyer belt and left the area as though he'd never been gone.

Green felt a sense of deflation, not exactly sadness, but not joy. His body gave no hint that within the next few days it would demand sleep for three or four days to adjust to Alaska time. New York was still four hours ahead of Alaska, so basically the old man had to adjust to a twelve-hour difference from Lisbon. The more David thought about it, the more he realized he was sad, but he couldn't put his finger on why.

CHAPTER 15

Manhattan, what has become of you?

The rest of this account of an old man's cabin fever and quarantine is closer to non-fiction than imagination. David and the author's travels through the streets from Penn Station to Port Authority and beyond coincide.

David's dilemma was how would he get to Buffalo to see his older son who had Covid, was given an intravenous dose of possibly Remdesivir. All David knew for sure was that after his son, Ari was diagnosed, he went to a hospital where the staff stuck a needle in his vein or was it subdural, he wasn't sure, and he sounded like death warmed over (what was that cliché all about). He stayed in the hospital for about three or four hours under close watch, The nurses did vitals every half hour during the procedure and after as well.

On the phone his son could barely speak, had a fever of about 103 and was in perilous shape. His friends came over, and he talked to them through a closed door. His dog, Moonshot, could play in the fenced in yard and sleep indoors, but Ari was in no shape to walk her, throw the ball for her to run after or do anything but wait for his symptoms to subside.

True to form his son thought he knew all the rules set by Governor Cuomo and when David got to Penn Station, he called his son but received no answer. That was not unusual. He probably was sleeping, and they'd agreed that both would not be scared that something bad had happened to either one. They would simply keep trying until success.

David asked a police officer in which direction Port Authority was so that he could buy a ticket from Greyhound to Buffalo. It may have been about midnight or close to it, US time. Figuring the old man in front of him just another soul without a home, the uniformed officer advised him to take a taxi because it was a good seven or eight blocks away. He didn't mention that the streets were no place for an elderly person.

That wasn't going to happen. Taxis were expensive in NYC, and some would take advantage of "foreigners". Who knew how much seven or eight blocks would cost?

David sat down for a short rest before he started for the Greyhound Station. He thought about the subway ride from JFK to Penn Station. The train had graffiti inside, outside, was dirty and the seats had knife slits on some of the seats. People were insulated from one another because all seemed focused on their Smart phones, barely looked up themselves or if in pairs seemed to whisper to each other.

Contrasts to the Tube in London were stark. The trains in London had no graffiti or torn seats, and in general people looked at one another and smiled, at least at him. When he asked for directions or an innocuous question, people seemed interested in helping.

So pointed in the right direction, David began to walk to Port Authority and the statue of Jackie Gleason who played Ralph Kramden on TV for many years. "An eight-foot-tall bronze statue of a jolly Jackie Gleason stands in front of Manhattan's midtown Port Authority Bus Terminal." He is dressed in his bus driver uniform with his lunch pail in his hand.

The show was called The Honeymooners during David's 11ᵗʰ and 12ᵗʰ grades. It ran from 1955-1956 and was loved by most TV viewers. Gleason played a bus driver in a metropolitan city living in Brooklyn. Alice his loving wife and Ed Norton played by Art Carney were mainstays in the series.

David remembered that Kramden treated his wife with abusive language, often raising his fist to her. Actually three different women played the part of Alice: Audrey Meadows, Sheila MacRae and Pert Kelton. Unfortunately, Kelton was caught up in the Anti Communist scare and was blackballed as an actress from stage and screen, thus the new wives.

David gleaned a lot of this information on the people who played in the Honeymooners from Goggle and realized that even in comedy, societal norms had changed and Kramden's treatment of his wife, would no longer be tolerated. Today many in the audiences would be enraged by Gleason's abusive language, threats, and his general means of dealing with sitcom challenges. He thought about the sit.com All in the Family and the way Carroll O'Conner treated his wife and daughter, for that matter everyone. Today many groups would be furious with that show as well. It was common that a wife took the blame for anything which angered her husband. No longer is that tolerated on the TV screen- thank something or another.

This made Green reflect on a woman who within the last year or so actually told him that she had been a bad girl and her husband had to give her a spanking. When she admitted this in a gathering in which David was a guest, he was mortified. Could this be in the here and now? The problem was that it was not her husband who glibly told this story, but rather his wife who saw no problem with deferring to her husband this way.

Ruth Bader Ginsburg would turn over in her grave. David laughed to himself; He didn't even know what this cliché meant. The woman had to be in her fifties and her husband in his sixties.

This memory led to David thinking about the Evangelical who told him her life story in about three minutes of her prostitution, living on the street and then finding Jesus, and this led to something he'd just read on Facebook which compared Scientists to Evangelicals. As he remembered it, Scientists read hundreds of books and say, "I know that I don't know and need to study more" while Christian Fundamentalists say, "I only need to read one book. I don't need to know anything else. I know everything I need to know." David shook his head in disbelief.

David was not comfortable with extremes on either side. Scientists could be snooty and dismissive of anyone who they felt was beneath them, while some, even many of the fundamentalists of all religions could be dogmatic, exclusionary, and even ready to kill for their beliefs.

David questioned how the two could be so different and what made them so. He shuttered when he questioned the differences in intelligence, education, family upbringing, intrinsic personality issues and even morality concerns.

He could go on about Lawrence Kohlberg's work on moral development and did some research on him. Kohlberg argued that "correct moral reasoning was the most significant factor in moral decision-making, and that correct moral reasoning would lead to ethical behavior". He believed that "individuals progress through stages of moral development just as they progress through stages of cognitive development."

For David, this was an invitation to do his own research and perhaps a survey of people who are Evangelicals, die hard Trump fans, and if possible the people who stormed the Capitol to seek their own brand of electoral justice versus people who might be religious but moderates in any perspective, college educated, and people who believed that America should be the bastion of invitation to all peoples to come and make a life for themselves and their families.

He quoted the first line of the poem on the Statute of Liberty, "Hand me your poor yearning to be free, I lift my lamp onto thee." The poem did not exclude people of color, religions other than Christianity, people that were different than Western European descendants or make any other distinctions. Emma Lazarus wrote the beautiful words on the Lady in the harbor.

David was aghast at the people he saw as he walked to the bus station. Street people, prostitutes, heavy duty partyers, kids dressed provocatively waiting to be hurt and an assortment of people like himself. He decided that if panhandlers approached him for money, he would beat them to the punch by asking for a handout before they could ask him. He almost looked lost, forlorn, and down and out. What he didn't want was someone to steal his suitcase or worse his backpack. He made his way past the statute of Jackie Gleason and found an open door.

He was going to buy a bus ticket to Buffalo and sit until the bus left New York City. He still did not know whether his son wanted him to come or not. He rarely knew what his son wanted or whether he really wanted his father to visit him. It was a painful truth which lived within David for many years and still did. The old man felt the same way about his other son. The difference was that he'd come to acceptance that their relationship might never be what he wished. Life promises us nothing but twists and turns. The Quarantine and Covid-19 proved that correct.

CHAPTER 16

Port Authority, a shadow of its old self

Port Authority used to be a fairly easy terminal to buy a bus ticket. Millions of people used the facility for their riding pleasure. After the attacks on the North and South Towers, that all changed and understandably so.

For instance, no longer was there a place where people could leave their luggage and pay by the hour. So tourists could not walk around Manhattan without the weight of suitcases and whatever else they might be carrying. This lasted for several years and then reopened for a brief time. It was an immense help for elderly and young as well.

Furthermore, one could wander the stores, the fast-food kiosks and buy a newspaper to sit and relax. The police were affable, courteous, and more than willing to be of help to people who needed advice of all kinds.

David's experience was that all of what preceded changed and that Port Authority changed into a horrendous experience. He could not find an entrance after trying several doors. When he did find one that was open, he could not find a Greyhound sales office or any other area to purchase a ticket. There were no employees to help him and even the sparce Port Authority Police seemed disinterested in helping anyone. They were there, it seemed, to make sure that no drunks, homeless, or pimps were causing any trouble. The bus station reminded David of a dank, smelly, jail cell he'd once visited long ago at the insistence of New York's finest. It was a civil rights protest for which he was arrested.

Greyhound was not opened, and he asked a man from the Middle East how he got a ticket. In halting English, the elderly gentleman said that the only way to get a ticket was on a Smart Phone or some other electronic means. He frowned, "Thank Allah, my son helped me."

It turned out that there was a bus going to Buffalo around 2 am in the morning and it was nearly ready to pull out. It was at Gate 52. David rushed to the Gate and found a lengthy line with a grossly overweight driver taking tickets. She was somewhat surly to the passengers, and he heard her say in a muffled voice something to the effect, "Why don't these people learn to speak English?" She didn't direct her comment at anyone in particular but compared to the bus drivers in England she was odious. Additionally, David heard some would be passenger ask if he could buy a ticket from her and she said, "No, You, can only get a ticket on-line and this bus is full and there ain't another one for six hours."

There was no attempt to have a second bus available for overflow. Someone standing off to the side asked her for help and she looked at him as if he was asking her for a hand- out. At the gate, there were perhaps ten seats available for sitting and they appeared to be for three or four gates. The seats were made of hard metal. As the bus began to fill, women with children got up and joined someone holding their place in line.

David sat down for a few minutes to think about his options. His Smart Phone was down to about 20% charge left and there were no electrical outlets that he could see to charge it.

But more importantly, he realized that he had no idea whether his son wanted him to come to see him. Additionally, sitting on these chairs was becoming more painful by the minute. He wondered whether that was Port Authority's way of keeping rift raft like David out of their "fine" bus terminal. It worked.

The bus to Buffalo began to pull out of its slip and he was left alone to contemplate his moves. He decided to return to Penn Station walking back the same way he had come. What was another eight blocks? Jet lag had not begun to take effect.

He meandered his way to the street level, found the 8th Ave. entrance that he had come in through and left Port Authority. Stopping at Jackie Gleason's statute for one final look, he realized that Gleason not only was rough on his wives in the sit com, but that he could not remember Gleason without an alcoholic drink in his hand in his other appearances on TV. In all, Gleason's persona was one of an alcoholic wife abuser. Not a great legacy in retrospect.

The walk back to the train station was the same except that he found a building which he had not seen before with comfortable benches in front, and he sat down and almost fell asleep. No one bothered him. Catching himself nodding off, he shook himself and got up. No time to have his backpack with his computer or suitcase stolen now when so close to the end of his "vacation". He laughed at the thought.

The same characters were on the street, perhaps with different faces, but their modus operandi had not changed. Prostitutes, pimps, drunks, homeless men and women, tourists wandering the streets looking for excitement as David went about doing his life hoping for the best. It meant different things to different folks. This time no one asked him for a hand-out, and he did not have to beat them to the punch by asking for one himself. He heard many sirens, but there were no police walking a beat, that he could see.

Penn Station was as busy as it had been when he got off the train from JFK. Port Authority police were all over the station and there seemed to be a sense of security that David definitely did not feel at the bus station or on the street. He imagined that more affluent people were at the train station than at the bus depot.

These cops looked like New York's finest, but their patches identified them as Port Authority police. They wore guns, had handcuffs and if not scrutinized would be mistaken as the New York police. The clientele at the train station was definitely different than that of the bus station. Middle class vs. poor, simple as that…And there was no comparison if one looked at the clientele at the airport either. Green felt a sense of despair and anger at what Capitalism wrought. He blamed

Capitalism for most of society's ills. Right or wrong, no one had ever made a convincing case otherwise.

David took a train back to JFK. He decided that if his son wanted him to come to Buffalo to see him, he would fly; If not, he would go home to Willow. He was tired and he felt old and vulnerable. He was after all within two days of his 83rd birthday.

At the airport he found a comfortable seat next to a fixture in the wall which permitted him to charge his phone. No one seemed to notice him, and he nodded off for a half hour. His phone was charged and that took a load off his mind. He set his watch for New York time while still on the plane from Lisbon. It was about 5am. Maybe he'd slept longer than he thought. Here and there small coffee shops were beginning to open for tourists and the like. Starbucks was opened and pilots and their crews were getting their morning fix.

David tried calling his son. Amazingly, the phone came to life on the first ring. David was elated. The upshot of the call was that Ari was adamant that David should not come to see him because he'd have to stay at a hotel, speak through a door and that he wasn't healthy enough to see anyone directly. David was in no shape to debate with him but assumed that having been vaccinated before the trip began, having a zillion Covid tests which were negative and, oh yes, wanting desperately to see his sick son would be enough for his son to want to see his dad as soon as he could. Not so! Maybe Ari which meant Lion in Hebrew, was looking out for his dad and David could find no fault with that.

David didn't want to argue with Ari. They had a better relationship at least on the telephone. That had taken years.

Maybe that's the way it would always be. Green believed that his son really believed that he was doing the right thing. But David's heart ached to hear that he wasn't wanted and that Ari rationalized his comments somehow.

They parted with terms of endearment and a promise that they would see each other when his son was no longer ill with Covid-19. For David, it was always the same. He racked his brain to be sure he wasn't being selfish, inconsiderate, self-serving. He didn't know how, but what was the use of arguing. It was Ari who was ill, not David and David had already switched to using his driver's license rather than his passport so no questions would ever be raised about quarantine or anything else.

It was easy to get lost in the thinking process. But it was easier to chalk it up to business as usual with his older son. When he checked his mail at home, he found a beautiful birthday card from Ari and later a wonderful Father's Day card. Go figure. Always look for the unexpected.

David thought about his reaction to the phone call and then it occurred to him that Ari's son left their apartment to go to Florida to live with his uncle, David's younger son so that he could go to college. That didn't work out and yet, his grandson stayed in Florida rather than go back to his dad's home. What was that cliché? "What goes around comes around." The old man couldn't remember if that were it or not, but his pain lifted slightly.

David knew lots of older guys, most of them veterans and many complained about unhappy relationships with their sons, and some had messed up conflicts with their daughters as well, not to mention their wives and girlfriends or boyfriends.

David lamented that it probably had to do with leaving his wife, their mom and then having to raise them when she died and doing a poor job of it. Another adage came to mind, "You reap what you sow." The thought descended upon David like a dark cloud.

CHAPTER 17

Home Sweet Home

David decided that he needed to go home to his four-legged children post haste. After his telephone call with his son, he could only imagine what Reba III, his German Shepherd, fox mix who adored her two- legged dad might be thinking with his being gone so long. On the other hand, he assumed that Jjay, his Kerelian and WuWu, the great grandmother wouldn't care much as long as they were fed, had plenty of water and a treat now and then.

David called Alaska Airlines from his seat at JFK and checked to see if he could use his mileage plan for a return to the last frontier. Luckily, he had plenty of miles left, and there was a seat all the way to Anchorage with a layover for about two hours in Seattle. He scooped it up and would be leaving JFK within three or four hours.

He thought again of his travels and compared himself to Ulysses in Homer's The Iliad. That was the epic poem by Homer of the king who spent years trying to get home from fighting in the Trojan Wars. David was too tired to be sure that he had it straight, but vaguely remembered about a king who traveled through thick and thin to return to his home, only remembered by his dog and a nurse. He'd read that somewhere. Then he wondered whether his kids would remember him, but he'd only been gone for a month. That was enough.

He slept all the way to SEA-TAC and couldn't remember any dreams, nightmares or if he even awoke when the flight attendants offered something to drink and gave the passengers a biscuit which always reminded David of the wafers offered parishioners for Communion when they were blessed by the priests in the Roman Catholic Church. Maybe the wafers were last rites just in case and maybe the attendants were clergy in drag.

He couldn't even remember whether he had to go to the bathroom during the flight. Maybe not, because upon leaving the plane, he rushed to the men's room and almost didn't make it in time. Luckily, the flight to Anchorage was three gates from where he deplaned from New York.

He stopped at a Starbucks and had his usual black coffee and a scone. This would have to tide him over until he got to Anchorage. The waiting area for the next flight to Anchorage was crowded with tourists waiting to see Russia's gift to the United States in 1867. Of course the U.S. paid for it, but America made out like the proverbial bandit in the sale. Almost one hundred years later, Alaska became the 49th State of the Union followed in the same year by Hawaii. Neither state was contiguous to the mainland and the other forty-eight states. But oh so different. Hawaii voted Democrat while Alaska was proud of its red neck Republican ties. When thinking about this, David often wondered why he loved it so. Flora and fauna, no doubt about it. And the dogs, the incredible dogs. They made humankind look so good regardless of politics.

David dwelled on the thought that since 1959 there had been no new states added to the country and now the District of Columbia and Puerto Rico were seriously being considered for statehood by many Americans. It was highly charged with Democrats and Republicans alike for and against the issues. David, having been born in D.C. was dedicated to statehood and felt that Puerto Rico would be treated a whole lot better by the Federal Government if a state. He felt that Rich Coast which was what Puerto Rico meant would not have suffered so at the hands of hurricanes had the territory been a state. Both had representation in the House of Representatives with one delegate each, but without a vote.

Additionally, most Americans probably did not know that Columbus decimated the Taino and Boroquin, the two Indian tribes on the island in his quest to find a sea route to the sub-continent India. David never could thank Howard Zinn enough for his writing of The Peoples History of the United States, Volume One and Two. Zinn wrote from the viewpoint of the losers in the America's quest for empire. David believed that all history was written from the perspective of the historian writing and not solely as a matter of fact and evidence. David smiled to himself and mused, "History is both non-fiction and fiction and taught as gospel." Children are rarely encouraged to challenge what they are made to read.

The plane to Anchorage was full. Tourists were coming out of their shells, their homes and living their dream of coming to see Denali, fish for Halibut and Salmon, see moose, bears, and pristine beauty unlike any where they resided. Covid was a reality, and many agreed to follow airline policy and wear masks on the flight, but some smarted at having to follow rules they disagreed with and felt to be arbitrary.

David met a fellow veteran, a combat grunt who'd earned a Bronze Star in Viet Nam. He spent a lifetime in the Service and retired with nearly 30 years in the Army. His wife was several years younger and beautiful and made necklaces and wristbands to commemorate deeds done for the country. They were like millions of Americans who felt about the Armed Forces like it were some sort of hallowed religion.

David didn't confront Joe and Donna, but as always, he made it clear that he was a Cold War veteran, had never killed anyone that he knew of and furthermore, did not want to harm anyone. From time to time, David went further and told people about Smedley Butler, his short work, *War is a Racket*, but he had no need to stand on a soap box with this nice couple.

David knew many anti-war veterans, Viet Nam Vets against the war, and loved some and admired many. But he also debated some of the people who belonged to groups like World Against All Wars, Pacificists who were just as adamant as the gun toting, America Love it or leave it yahoos. He believed that Hitler, Mussolini, Tojo and other Fascists needed to be stopped at all costs, but Viet Nam was a deceit from the beginning. He doubted the sincerity of those who vilified Israel and its treatment of Palestine because he believed many were simply out and out Jew haters. Not all though... Enough said.

While in Seattle, David called his favorite hotel in Anchorage, made a reservation to pay top dollar for one it its bigger and more elegant rooms and spend the evening there. He decided to give himself a present for his birthday. Tomorrow he would be a year older legitimately. He would no longer explain that in Viet Nam he was already 83 because they viewed age based on conception or at least that's what he thought they meant.

Again at the airport in Anchorage, he was not asked any questions about Covid, no inquiries of where he'd been for the last month nor did they insist on a rapid test. It was almost as though Alaska had never been hit with the pandemic. See no evil, hear no evil, speak no evil, seemed to be their unspoken mantra.

David gave his calling card to several people on the flight and invited them to visit him in his small town while they were touring, but none of them ever called enroute to Denali or Fairbanks.

However, in the hotel, he had an interesting experience. On Sunday, May 23rd, he went down to the lobby for his breakfast that was part of the fare at the hotel. A woman approximately 70 years old was eating alone and he joined her. She was moving from the Mat-Su to Fairbanks area, was with her son in an RV, but he was not at the breakfast table.

David never really understood why she was moving, but she was a comely woman, interesting at first glance and friendly. So he gave her a card and told her to give a call if and when she came through Willow. She did a few days later and wanted to come over to his house with the RV and her son. The old man's ears began to burn, a sign of heightened awareness of 'all is not well.' As it turned out, David was about to do a volunteer gig with his Community Emergency Response Team, (CERT), and he would not be available. He never heard from her again.

Jake and Molly, two wonderful people that David knew from his Veterans group allowed David to leave his car at their home while he traveled. Jake served in Nam as a Special Forces operative and came home only to have a stroke which left him with problems for the rest of his life. Molly, like David, was a Diabetic, but she took it a lot more seriously than David.

Jake was a scholar dedicated to America ending its empire and need to control the world. He had loads of friends, both veteran and nonveteran and was involved in think tanks dedicated to peace and social justice. David and Jake handed out newspapers dedicated to peace sent from the East Coast and worked for a while on a project to keep business interests from privatizing the Veterans Administration.

Molly served as an officer of a rehabilitation hospital/school for Vietnamese young people affected by Agent Orange and other defoliates that harmed Vietnamese and Americans alike. They spent many weeks in Viet Nam after the war doing volunteer work on behalf of the youth and school employees. In David's opinion these were two of the finest people he knew anywhere in the world.

On Sunday morning, now fully 83 years old, David drove back to his home, stopped for a few groceries on the way and had decided to pick up his children who were vacationing for the month with thirteen dogs destined for Iditarod fame in the future. David's friend Suzanne and her husband brought the dogs home and he and his children reunited with glee and tails wagging, even David's.

He remembered the incident while in Basic Training. Thus ended the Quarantine vacation that was never supposed to be.

David spent the first three days, sleeping off and on, trying to reset his brain's clock to Alaskan time, some twelve hours earlier than Portuguese time.

He never got to North Africa, never found his old friend/adversary who may have financed the bombing of a train in Spain, but David would never know for sure. All Green could think of was The Rain in Spain from My Fair Lady. But it rhymed with Train which helped to remain in his memory. Nothing would ever be the same, but then, again, nothing ever is.

Final Thoughts

Ten Thoughts on How to Get to your 100th Birthday in one piece

David Green had a lot of time to think while serving his time in quarantine. He thought about a life well spent and what his future looked like when he would be all of 83 years old.

Nosed pressed against the windowpane looking at the gigantic train station and the castle built in the nineteenth century, the throngs of people young and old who floated in and out of view in the sunlight and days of chilly rain, winds and cloudiness all melded together in his mind. These days and the following trips to Oxford, Bournemouth, Lisbon and even the streets of Manhattan provided David with thoughts he never had before.

From it all he decided to write what could be considered a codicil of sorts, a list of ten ideas for elders to live by in hope of making their lives work for them. He read many how to books on how to be successful, how to make a difference, and how to be happy, how to be rich and how to be a leader. None of them were specifically written for those in his age range and in David's mind too late anyway.

David sat down, realized that he had been considering this while he drove, in his sleep, and in conversations which he had with friends. He decided to put them to paper to share them with his cohort.

1. To live a century, get through the 80's and 90's having done life as though you were in your 50's and 60's.
2. Read the Gestalt Prayer (which is not a spiritual prayer) at least once a week and think about it.
3. Do something outside your comfort zone at least once a month. It will broaden your horizons and you'll have something to talk about to your old friends and family.
4. There is something to being your own best friend. It gets one through loneliness, moments of normal despair and self- pity.
5. If you hang on to old angers toward others, re-evaluate the value of hanging onto anything. Hanging on is just not worth the effort and promotes living in the past.
6. If you are physically able, see the world. Become a citizen of the world. We are one of 7 billion people. Rough it a bit rather than taking cruises. (Example- Take the Alaskan Marine Ferry up to the Last Frontier from Bellingham, WA. and sleep on wooden benches out to Dutch Harbor in the Aleutian Chain).
7. Always think you are one year older than you are. You'll get to the century mark quicker.
8. Never, ever, pee behind your dog sled. Always pee in front of your team. That way if they try to run without you, you can pull up your pants, hop on your sled and mush on. (Submitted by a younger woman musher

who is sixty years old, Julie Nelson). She is an amazing woman.

9. Live in the here and now because it is all we have anyway. The Buddhist monk was right. Now get on with life! Keep on keeping on!

10. Disregard the above nine and make your own.

Printed in the United States
by Baker & Taylor Publisher Services